MODERN SYRIAN SHORT STORIES

MODERN SYRIAN SHORT STORIES

Translated by Michel G. Azrak
Revised by M.J.L. Young

3CP

An Original by Three Continents

©1988 Michel Azrak & M.J.L. Young

Three Continents Press
1636 Connecticut Avenue, N.W.
Washington, DC 20009

Library of Congress Cataloging-in-Publication Data

Modern Syrian short stories.
    1. Short stories, Arabic—Syria—Translations into
English.   2. Short stories, English—Translations from
Arabic.   3. Short stories, Arabic—20th century—
Translations into English.   I. Azrak, Michel G.
II. Young, M. J. L.
PJ7695.E8M6   1988   892'.73'010895691   86-51002
ISBN 0-89410-440-3
ISBN 0-89410-441-1 (pbk.)

Cover art by Max Winkler
©1988 Three Continents Press

Foreword

The Arabs have been masters of the art of story telling since at least the time of the *Thousand and One Nights,* and it is therefore not surprising that in modern days they have produced a rich literary harvest in the field of the short story.

Syria in particular has produced some outstanding writers in this field, and the present collection of eighteen stories has been selected with a view to giving the English reader some idea of the range of modern Syrian fiction.

We have here stories ranging from the comic (John Alexan) to the macabre (Haydar Haydar) and the ghost story (Nabil Sulayman)—a literary bouquet of great freshness and variety.

M.G.A.
Aleppo, 1986

To my wife Mona, and my daughter Georgina

TABLE OF CONTENTS

INTRODUCTION

The renaissance of Arabic literature in the nineteenth century involved not only a rediscovery and appreciation of the rich legacy of medieval Arabic, but also the adoption of three European genres of imaginative literature—the drama, the novel, and the short story—which, in spite of having had somewhat remote forerunners in Arabic literature in the Middle Ages, were substantially new introductions to the Arabic-speaking world under the influence of the West.

Of these new genres the short story has had the widest influence, and it is the most popular of all forms of fictional writing among Arab authors today. Dr. Abd al-Salam al-Ujayli, one of whose stories appears in the present collection, has pointed out that the short story has today replaced the classical Arab ode as the central genre of Arabic literature, and the very large numbers of stories published throughout the Arab countries certainly bear this out.

From modest beginnings in the nineteenth century, the Arabic short story developed rapidly after the First World War, but only since the Second World War can it be said to have reached a stage of maturity. Since then it has developed in many different directions, including those of realism, symbolism, social criticism, nationalism, surrealism, and the absurd.

Syrian writers have been among the most prominent in this literary field, and have produced some of the leading short-story writers in modern Arabic literature.

The origins of the Syrian short story can be traced to before the First World War, but the effective beginnings of the genre in Syria were in the 1930s. By about 1950, the short story was well established as a

1

literary medium, and the earlier stories of such writers as Abd al-Salam al-Ujayli, Fu'ad al-Shayib, and Muzaffar Sultan had appeared.

The period from about 1950 onward was one of strong European literary influences, particularly French and Russian, but including also some English and German influences. This was also the time of the emergence of a prominent Syrian middle class. Since the 1960s there has been increasing experimentation and innovation in the Syrian short story, and among the new themes which have entered into its subject matter have been those of social oppression, the problem of Palestine, and the search for true ethical values.

About half the stories in the present collection have some element of social observation or criticism. This appears most clearly in Ulfat al-Idlibi's "The Women's Baths," in which the description of the old-fashioned women's baths of Arab traditional life takes up the bulk of the story, which has the simplest of plots. This story is typical of the fiction of Ulfat al-Idlibi, a realist who usually employs a direct, straightforward form of narrative with events related in chronological order. Her stories are derived from the reality of everyday life, although her connections with upper-class circles are often apparent in her fiction.

In the stories by Abdullah Abid ("Our Fighting Cock") and John Alexan ("The Locusts"), we have glimpses of the social background of the Syrian countryside, together with something of its sly humor, and we find something of the same traditional setting and the same sly humor in Fadil al-Siba'i's story "An Accident at 'The Palace of Happiness.'" All three of these authors are realists who are of the generation which came to prominence after the Second World War.

In George Sālim's story "The Power of Darkness" we have a grim criticism of a police state and the suppression of free speech. George Sālim, who died at the early age of 43, is one of the most remarkable of modern Syrian writers, and one whose collected short stories will undoubtedly be eventually translated in full. Nearly all of his stories are symbolic, and they are written in a spare, precise style which leaves a lasting impression on the reader. The symbolic character of his fiction is emphasized by the fact that he does not give his characters names, and frequently his stories take the form of allegories concerned with the ultimate questions: the significance of human life and striving, man's inevitable end, the apparent helplessness of the individual against the world. The influence of Franz Kafka is often evident in his work.

Criticism of a different kind is the theme of the longest piece in this collection, "Madness" by Dr. Abd al-Salam al-Ujayli, which treats of the futility and pettiness of private lives. The social realism of the narrative has in addition a symbolic aspect which is brought out by the characters themselves toward the conclusion. This story is but one item of a prolific literary output which spans nearly 50 years, and which has made Dr. Ujayli one of the best-known contemporary Syrian authors. The bibliography compiled by Mustafa Shahhadah of those of his works which appeared in print between 1937 and 1972 lists 450 items. These include poetry, short stories, novels, essays, travel books, and a great number of contributions to journals and periodicals. He has also contributed with success to the medieval Arabic literary genre of the *maqamah,* a form of dramatic anecdote in rhymed prose, which usually has satire or social criticism as its aim.

The stories of Sa'id Huraniyyah arise from a deep feeling of affection for suffering humanity and an attitude of reverence for the earth and the natural world. This appears in his story "Another Hard Winter." The weakness which assails the tree in this story, threatening it with death, is a symbol for the calamities which threaten all living things. In Sa'id Huraniyyah's work in general we find a revolt against the past and its bad conditions, against tyrannical families and harsh parents; Huraniyyah is usually described as a socialist realist.

Two love stories—or rather stories of thwarted love—appear in this collection. "Old Enough to Be Your Father" is a typical example of the work of Ghadah al-Saman, whose fiction began to appear in the 1960s, and who is one of the leading Syrian women writers today. She is a realist, whose concern with the fate of human beings takes as its starting point the description of ways of behavior, morals, and the impact of new ways of life. "East is East" is an example of the work of one of the pioneers of the modern Syrian short story, Fu'ad al-Shayib. Although he only published one collection of short stories (*Tarikh Jarah,* 1944), he left an enduring mark on the art of the realistic narrative in Syria.

Stories which pose questions regarding the reality of personal identity are those by Walid Ikhlasi ("Wondering Who . . .") and Colette Khuri ("Sarab"). "Wondering Who" is the study of a man with a split personality, whose "Mr. Hyde" commits a murder, unknown to "Dr. Jekyll." This theme is characteristic of the work of Walid Ikhlasi, many of whose short stories are concerned with the question of personal identity. The scope of his literary contributions, however, goes far beyond this; they range from studies in surrealistic impressionism to realistic narratives, and he has even written some effective animal fables. Ikhlasi is a modernist in the literary sense of the term, i.e. an individualist who starts from a basic refusal to accept existing values, and whose vision of a confused human existence is reflected in his use of literary devices such as interior monologue and stream-of-consciousness.

Colette Khuri, like Ghadah al-Saman, is representative of the

4

Syrian women writers who came to prominence in the 1960s. In most of her work she is a realist writer who is particularly noteworthy for her ability to analyze the middle-class environment of Syrian city life, and the subjects of her stories generally have a coloring of social background. Her story "Sarab" describes the bewilderment of a man met unexpectedly by a girl who has been waiting for him for a year; yet he is convinced he cannot possibly have ever known this girl at any time in his life, and reacts to her as a total stranger.

In the three stories "The Destroyer of Families," "The Rain," and "The Butterfly Collector," by Sabah Muhyi 'l-Din, Yasin Rifa'iyyah, and Muzaffar Sultan, respectively, we have three tales which are realistic throughout in form, but which in each case include a single supernatural element which is either obviously so, as in the case of the baleful ring in "The Destroyer of Families," or which has more than a suggestion of the supernatural about it, as in the case of the fall of rain in "The Rain" and the obsession for killing butterflies in "The Butterfly Collector."

Sabah Muhyi 'l-Din's story is a tale in the direct tradition of the *Thousand and One Nights,* a celebrated work of medieval Arabic literature which is mentioned by one of the characters in this story. "The Rain" has also something of the marvels of the *Thousand and One Nights* about it, although here the setting is a rural one. The supernatural element in Muzaffar Sultan's story "The Butterfly Collector" is more subtle, in that the demonic nature of the boy's urge to hunt butterflies is implied rather than stated, and the surface appearance of the story is one of realism.

Nabil Sulayman's ghost story "The Wrath of Shaykh Muhammad al-Ajami" is overtly supernatural, with the appearance of a phantom as its central event.

The remaining stories in this collection are ones which enter into the realm of surrealistic horror, and which also contain symbolic elements: "The Ants and the Qat" by Haydar Haydar, "The Ablution" by Hani al-Rahib, and "The Thunderbolt" by Zakariyya Tamir. In the first of these, the hero's dreams of grandeur are thwarted by his being killed by ants; in the second, the hero's desire to be washed clean ends with his being washed by blood; and in the third, a petulant schoolboy destroys everything with an atomic bomb.

Zakariyya Tamir in particular is notable for the individualistic, subjective trend in his stories, which sometimes tend to expressionism and have elements of the absurd. In general his work deals with failure, futility, and a disgust for the actualities of life, and this pessimism can to some extent be traced to the influence of Camus and Sartre.

Taking a very broad view of literary history over the last 40 years, we can trace in the development of the Syrian short story since the Second World War a general change from the construction of stories around actions and events, to a more static form in which the portrayal of atmosphere is the writer's main concern; it is hoped that the present collection goes some way toward illustrating some of the facets of this literary development.

M.J.L.Y.
Leeds, 1986

OUR FIGHTING COCK

Abdullah Abid

❧❧

WHEN I HAD ASSEMBLED the boys of our village quarter, and the group which was going to the village of al-Darf was complete, I said: "Right, let's go!"

They replied: "Let's go!"

Ibrahim, a supercilious boy with a snub nose and dishevelled hair, spoke: "We seem to have forgotten about the cock!"

I replied: "Of course we haven't! How could we forget it when it's the whole purpose of our trip to al-Darf?"

He rejoined: "Maybe we have forgotten something else besides the cock?" He turned to Nadim. "Show me your catapult!"

Nadim pulled his catapult out of his pocket and held it up. "Here it is!"

"And the stones?"

"Here are the stones."

Then he searched out Sulayman from the front of the group and asked him: "Where is your catapult?"

Sulayman struck his forehead in exasperation: "Oh!—I've left it at home!"

Ibrahim's lips curled slightly as he said without pursuing his victory: "Well, go and fetch it." And no sooner had Sulayman set off at a run toward his house than he called after him: "Don't forget the bullets!"

Everyone took up Ibrahim's rather shrill cry, which in no way matched the bulkiness of his body or his status as leader of war operations between us and the other boys: "He says don't forget the bullets!"

By "bullets" was meant of course stones for the catapults. But at

7

that time it would have been more fitting to call them "shells," for the truth of the matter is that when boys fight with each other a catapult has the same function as a cannon in grown-up fights. At all events, after Ibrahim had inspected our arsenal, including catapults, slings, and stones, I gave the signal to move off. Final authority was mine. I was the son of the village mayor.

So we set off toward the village of al-Darf, which a man can reach in twenty minutes, if he walks, or ten minutes if he is mounted. Of course, none of us had mounts for this journey, although some of us could have ridden on beasts belonging to our families. But we were afraid of possible dire consequences.

The lads of al-Darf had defeated us heavily five days ago in a football match. This was not attributable to any weakness in our players, but was due to lack of impartiality on the part of the referee. When they refused a return match, we thought up another way of getting our revenge. Negotiations took place to arrange a cock-fight between a cock from our side and one from theirs. Defeat had left a very bitter taste in our mouths, but we were sure our cock would win.

He was a young bird with a sturdy body, long legs and neck, and multi-colored feathers, and his head was crowned with a beautiful crimson comb.

Contrary to the well-known habit of cocks, he would peck every hen that approached the chicken food when he was partaking of his own meal. Indeed, the hens had to offer him every tasty, whole grain which he himself had overlooked: so much so that he no longer gave himself the trouble of scratching around for his food. In this way he put on layer after layer of flesh. The hens bore him no grudge, for they had grown used to his behavior, and had conditioned themselves accordingly. Fowls at times behave like men. Was he not *their* cock, their defender? They therefore withdrew until he had finished his meal, and slept on a perch lower than his, so that he might enjoy his sleep on the highest perch in the hen-coop.

The hens would gaze at him proudly when he strutted in front of them, gorgeous and elegant with his plumage glinting silver and gold, especially when he stirred in the mornings to wake up the sleeping village with his loud, long, sustained crowing, which had a short, hoarse passage followed by a long note which breathed authority and bespoke pride and condescension. In fact his voice was one of the finest among all the roosters our village had known for many years, as the older folk of the village affirmed. He was the finest cock to be born after those years of drought which had plagued the area and decimated the cockerel population. Beautiful multi-colored plumage, perfect health, a voice which assaulted the ears. Just let them wait, those boys of al-Darf, we were coming for them. They had better mobilize every fighting cock in their village.

When we reached the frontiers of al-Darf we dispatched a messenger to the boys of the village demanding that they produce their cock.

Ibrahim had chosen a lush green meadow to be the battleground for the fighting cocks. When one of the comrades wildly proclaimed: "We must crush them in the very center of the village and make them complete laughingstocks!" Ibrahim answered him with the gravity of a general, responsible for a body of men, who knew precisely what to do in these circumstances: "From the point of view of capacity, this meadow will fulfill our purpose perfectly, since it can take every one of the villagers. There is no open space in the village which is big enough for a crowd of people like this. Quite apart from that the meadow is at the meeting point of roads from several other villages."

He paused for this to sink in, and added: "I hope you understand my point."

Our lads looked at each other and broad smiles spread over our faces. Once again Ibrahim had given proof of his unchallenged ability as leader. And his genius went even further, for he continued: "Look at these rocks."

We looked in the direction of the rocks without at first understanding the import of what he said, but he went on: "These rocks are on the path back to our village. When we have achieved our tremendous victory, they will be just the right place to lie in ambush, if the al-Darf boys are tempted by the idea of having a set-to with us to avenge their cock's defeat. They would be completely at the mercy of our slings and catapults."

This plan caused some of us to dance about with enthusiasm, while others leaped in the air. In general this idea received overwhelming approval, in spite of the fear expressed by those with sticks that this strategy would not enable them to close with the enemy, and would thus render their weapons ineffective.

In any event we did not have long to wait, as the lads of al-Darf soon arrived carrying their cock in a covered cage, bringing with them a crowd of supporters. A number of passers-by, on their way to neighboring villages, joined the throng, which by now was forming a large ring around the meadow.

Betting started among the spectators, which became brisker and more frenzied as the two cocks were released. Most of the bets were laid on our cock: without a doubt our reputation stood very high in the area.

The two cocks began to circle around the ring, occasionally turning toward the crowd and crowing defiantly. Each one had his own vocal register and his own way of showing off. Our cock's crowing was like a keen blade—one might say it was like a knife piercing the very heart.

And if we add to his sharp, strident voice his strapping build, sturdy body and splendid proportions, then the final outcome should have been clear to everyone right from the beginning.

Yes, everyone with eyes in his head could see the vast difference in bodily fitness between the two cocks. Our cock strutted in a burnished plumage of splendid colors, and exuded vitality and strength. The cock of the al-Darf lads by contrast was black and scrawny, and the skin of its neck was bare. His comb was small and dark red in color, his beak was yellow, and his eyes were drowsy and somnolent. In short, he was a very ordinary cock, if not downright insignificant, in comparison with ours.

Our cock circled twice and displayed his feathers. His comb stood stiffly erect and glowed crimson with rage. The other cock retreated cowering before him and circled warily from a distance. It was clear that they were both weighing each other up and looking for points of weakness in their adversary which would give openings for attack, while each of them was trying to provoke fear in the heart of his opponent.

One of our rivals shouted: "Your cock is just a bird for show!" to which someone on our side retorted: "Showing off is the way to put fear into the heart of your cowardly cock!"

"You can't put fear into the heart of a real cock!"

One of our lads responded: "Do you think your cock is worth calling a cock?"

Someone on the other side shouted: "What counts is action!"

"What counts is the outcome, and the outcome of this match is as plain as the nose on your face!"

Someone else backed this up with: "Do you think this is a football match, you Darfites? You only got the better of us last week by having a corrupt referee!"

Another followed with: "You're going to pay for last week's business, and cough up your fake victory with blood and feathers!"

"Do their cocks have any feathers?"

"All right then, we'll put out their eyes!"

"But their cocks' eyes are so sleepy and drowsy they look as if they don't have any eyes!"

"Fine, then we'll rub their combs in the dust!"

"But their cocks don't have any combs."

"In that case why do they bother to call their cocks 'cocks' at all?"

All the members of our party laughed uproariously. Excitement among the crowd increased as they swayed first one way and then another to follow the maneuverings of the two fighting cocks as they advanced and retreated.

Our cock advanced, ruffling up the feathers on his outstretched neck until they resembled the mane of a young lion; his eyes flashed and reddened. He flapped his superb wings twice, revealing the beautiful plumage beneath them, and gave voice to his menacing war cry. Even in the hen-coop he was spruce and handsome. But he looked incomparable on the field of battle.

A voice was heard: "I told you he was only fit for a bird-show."

One of our rivals agreed: "Good grief! This cock is no good! He's only fit to strut around among his hens!"

In fact our cock had cornered his opponent, who continued to retreat before him, so that we were quite sure he was about to finish him off. But then the black cock suddenly pounced on ours and proceeded to peck him about the head, so that he lost some feathers.

One of our cock's supporters shouted: "That's his last throw! The black cock has dug his own grave! If he wants to get vicious let him have a taste of what he deserves for his own stupidity! The big cock is just playing with him. If he wanted he could knock him straight down!"

"Then why doesn't he knock him down?"

"Just you wait and he'll peck his eyes out!"

Our cock stretched out his neck and crowed with rage: he had received a blow which made the blood run. So much the worse for the black cock! Let him pay the full price for his temerity! The feathers of thoroughbred fighting cocks do not fly for nothing, nor is their blood shed in vain.

But the black cock swiftly descended upon his opponent with several sharp pecks on his comb. The blood began to flow. Great heavens! Threats were no longer having any effect on him. "Come on, you fine fellow, finish him off! It's no use being soft with moth-eaten birds like this one!"

But alack and alas! The black cock continued to attack and our cock continued to retreat. The brilliant feathers went on flying and the blood continued to flow. Fresh parts of our cock were exposed to concentrated pecking. When the black cock had mutilated his elegant comb he went on to his eyes and then his neck.

Someone exclaimed: "Show birds are no good as fighting cocks!"

Another voice shouted: "The real fighting cock attacks like a hawk and circles his opponent like a spinning wheel."

The voices of some of the older inhabitants of al-Darf were raised: "Boys, you should not be so boastful. Don't challenge other people's fighting cocks with cocks spoiled by over-feeding!"

Someone else cried out: "What a pity! He's a fine bird and there's no cock that can touch him for crowing, but he's no fighter. Just imagine if he had the good points of the black cock as well, or vice-versa!"

Another spectator reproved him sententiously: "Don't presume upon God's divine wisdom. Only God is perfect."

And in truth our cock's appearance had been completely disfigured, while the loud crowing with which he had begun the contest became fainter and fainter until it was reduced to a croak.

But the strange thing was that when he was returned to the hen-coop in his bedraggled condition, he proceeded to swagger about in front of the hens. And an even stranger thing was that the hens gave way before him as usual when he proceeded to peck at his food.

THE LOCUSTS

John Alexan

HAMDAN LEANED AGAINST THE CLAY WALL of his room and stretched out his legs in front of him; then he closed his eyes and proceeded to think . . .

For days he had been groping through the strands of a net of contradictory thoughts: "Why does Salman want to challenge me? How can I get the better of him? His peep-show is new, and is painted bright blue; it is decorated with colored lamps and glass balls and shiny mirrors and has four peep-holes for viewing, while my peep-show is twenty years old and is unpainted, and it has no lamps or mirrors, and it has only three peep-holes. Salman will without doubt show new colored pictures, not like my old worn-out pictures which the country people have seen so often they are tired of them . . . Oh good Lord . . . what am I to do? How can I face Salman's competition? How can I get the better of him?"

* * *

Those unacquainted with the story of Hamdan will not realize the crushing nature of the misfortune which had overcome him. It began when he found out that Salman was going to compete with him for his source of livelihood. For twenty years he had been setting off for the villages of the Eastern Province with his peep-show. Through its peep-holes he would show pictures he took from magazines. The country children, and sometimes the grown-ups, would rush to look into it. They would give him money, or a box of wheat-grain, or a pound of raw cotton, or some cereals, depending on the season, for he called on them in early June when the grain harvest was beginning and in the early

13

days of autumn, when the cotton harvest was in full swing.

At the end of these two seasons he would return to his small village nestling on the right bank of the Orontes, where he would live quietly and contentedly for the remaining months of the year on what he had collected.

This was how his life had proceeded for twenty years, like the irrigation canal near his village, which ran its uniform course, its waters neither hastening nor slackening, neither overflowing nor having their level raised by flooding. He was content to live by this seasonal livelihood. He did not want to bear responsibility for any other person, and he had not ventured into marriage, in spite of his age, which was approaching fifty. But he had never imagined that a serious competitor would suddenly appear in the field to preoccupy his mind and cast a shadow over his existence, at a time when he was preparing to set off for the Eastern Province at the beginning of a new season. Moreover, he had never dreamed that his competitor would be this very Salman, for he had known Salman, a seller of sesame sweets, for more than ten years, and his living was by no means a bad one: so why should he start to compete with him?

He went to see him.

"Why do you want to compete with me, Salman?"

Salman replied, while regarding his new peep-show with studied admiration and polishing one of its mirrors with the palm of his hand: "I am not competing with anyone. God's earth is wide and every man's living comes from Heaven . . ."

"But aren't you going to the Eastern Province? That is my province."

Salman's reply betrayed a tone of irritation: "*Your* province? And when was a *firman* issued making you the owner of the Eastern Province? It is open for anyone wishing to make his living there, so be sensible and get on with earning your own crust of bread."

Hamdan replied in an abject tone: "But my peep-show cannot compete with your new one, and I cannot afford to buy one like it. Anyway, you are a sweetmeat seller; so why do you want to deprive me of the living for which I have striven every season for twenty years?"

Wishing to end the conversation, Salman retorted: "Listen to me, Hamdan. All I've got to say is this: I am not competing with anyone. I am free to choose whatever way of life I like. If you wanted to sell sweets I should not try to stop you or accuse you of attacking my source of livelihood. Just leave me alone and don't start an open row between us . . ."

*   *   *

Hamdan returned home with a worried frown. The matter was out of his hands. He had been unable to induce Salman to give up his intentions, and he was unable to afford a new peep-show. What was he to do?

The only thing to do was to accept the competition. He would challenge Salman with his blue-colored peep-show, with its mirrors and four peep-holes. Yes, he would accept the challenge. He would show the villagers of the Eastern Province better pictures than those which Salman was going to show, even if Salman showed the most outstanding colored pictures from the very best magazines . . . yes . . . he would look for new kinds of pictures, which would make the country folk rush to him and ignore Salman's peep-show.

The last hours of the night were past and Hamdan was still thinking. Then at last he had the solution. He clapped his hands and jumped in the air. His joyful laugh almost dislocated his jaws. He had hit upon the means to compete with Salman successfully. "You will see, Salman, what a failure you are going to have . . . I shall make you put your peep-show up for sale at the lowest price imaginable, and you will find no buyers . . . you will get angry and smash it up and throw it on the fire, and then you'll come back to the village defeated to sit behind your tray of sesame sweets!"

In the morning Hamdan set off in the village bus to the county town. As soon as he got there he rushed to the Agricultural Center and asked to see the director. The porter tried unsuccessfully to prevent him from seeing him until he had learned the purpose of his call, but Hamdan insisted that the matter should be divulged to no one. This was so that it should not come to the ears of Salman, who would then copy him. All he would say to the porter was: "The matter is important. I must discuss it personally with the director."

When at last he was alone with the director in his office he said: "Everyone in the Eastern Province is worried, as they are expecting an attack of locusts there, now that the swarms have reached the desert areas. I've heard that you are preparing educational materials and instructions with explanatory pictures for fighting the locusts, for the use of farmers. I have a peep-show which I take around the Eastern Province throughout the harvest season: would you give me some of these pictures showing how to combat the locusts, so that I can show them to the people there before the locusts arrive? After all, I would be helping you in your job of educating the farmers."

Hamdan had not expected the director of the Agricultural Center to be so enthusiastic about his proposal; in fact he was delighted with the idea and congratulated him for it. He brought out a great pile of pictures and presented them to him with the compliments and thanks of the Center, and promised him an honorarium at the end of the season.

Before leaving the director's office, Hamdan said: "Would you grant me a special favor?"

The director replied: "Certainly. What is it?"

He answered: "I would like this matter to remain just between us . . . would you promise me that?"

The director laughed. "By all means!"

Hamdan returned to his village, went into his room, and locked the door. He spread out the pictures on the mat, got some scissors and trimmed them all to one size. Then he proceeded to stick them onto a tape with boiled starch, talking to himself as he did so: "You're amazing, Hamdan, you're a genius. You're going to make Salman bite his nails in vexation for the day he stopped selling sweetmeats and bought his blue peep-show to compete with you. I'll make him come on bended knee asking forgiveness. I won't even let him start his show. I'll set up my peep-show next to his and call out: 'Ladies and gentlemen . . . farmers . . . villagers! The locusts coming from the desert are threatening your crops. They are threatening your children and families with starvation. Their swarms will soon be here. So turn aside from your pleasures and come over here to me: I have prepared for you in this modest peep-show a complete reel of pictures showing you how to combat the locust swarms . . . Take no notice of these fripperies and silly pictures, ladies and gentlemen; cast away your apathy and indifference! This is a time for serious action! You should all take a look at my peep-show, because you will all be involved in facing the attack of the locusts. These pictures will surprise you. They will teach you—young and old, men and women—they will teach you all effective ways of fighting the locusts. This peep-show will help you to save your crops. Otherwise you are going to starve and your fields will be nothing but food for the locusts, which are already on their way. The latest news is that they will be here very shortly. So draw near and do not miss this opportunity!

'Even if the locusts do not land on your crops, the pictures will provide useful guidance for the future. Ladies! Gentlemen! Children! Hamdan has been among you for twenty seasons and feels that you are his family . . . his brothers . . . his clan. He is no stranger among you. He is not so much concerned for his own profit as for the future of your crops.

'Step right up, brothers! I could have brought you a new, shiny peep-show—colored blue with shiny mirrors and four peep-holes. I could have shown you color pictures, but instead I wanted to be of service. Consequently I made great efforts to obtain these pictures for you which will show you how to fight the locusts. Step right up, brothers! Step right up! Hamdan will save your harvest! Hamdan is your brother! And your servant! Step this way! This way to the modest, but profitable, peep-show! Step up, step up!' ''

* * *

There was a month to go before the harvest. Hamdan preferred to spend it in his room; he did not wish to mix with people for fear his tongue might let slip something about the pictures, and the information might then reach Salman, who would steal his idea and the harvest would be lost . . .

He kept spreading out the reel of pictures in front of him and composing vivid commentaries on each one, until he had learned all of it by heart. He got to know the position of each picture on the length of tape and what to say about them. Day after day he was on the alert for news about what Salman was doing, for he did not wish to set off before him, or later . . . he wanted to let the blow fall on the very first day.

The bus only ran to the Eastern Province once a week, and so he arranged with the man at the garage to let him know the time of his rival's departure, so that he could get to the Province at the same time.

The plan worked well. The garage man Abud came running: "Hurry up! Salman has brought his peep-show and stowed it on top of the bus. He's leaving in an hour."

Hamdan immediately got up, put his provisions into a bag, and placed the tape with its pictures into his breast pocket to make sure no one should steal them. Then he hoisted the peep-show onto his shoulder and set off for the garage. He supervised the securing of the peep-show on the top of the bus beside that of his rival, and before climbing down he couldn't resist scratching Salman's peep-show with a small piece of iron concealed in his hand.

As the bus set off, Salman turned his head to the right, and to his surprise Hamdan was sitting there. He had not realized that Hamdan had learned of his time of departure. Nevertheless he gave him a greeting and inquired about his peep-show. Hamdan replied: "It is entertaining your peep-show. It would have pained it to have left yours alone on the luggage rack."

Salman retorted: "I hope you've taught your peep-show how to behave in polite company, because if it lets drop an unseemly word it will get such a slap from my new peep-show that your worm-eaten box will fly in all directions."

"Rest assured, my friend—my peep-show is well-mannered because it comes of a good family. It has lived among the people for twenty years, and is one of them. That's why they are more fond of it than they will be of some strange peep-show which is unfamiliar to them."

"If you had seen the collection of colored pictures which I am going to exhibit you would ask the driver to take you back to the village!"

"The Lord will provide, Salman. Anyway, you will have my answer when we arrive."

Salman returned: "Don't worry—I shan't be ungenerous toward you. When the people come rushing up to my new peep-show, I shall ask them to throw you a few coppers; I won't let you just stand there miserably with your box, watching your customers desert you."

Salman then put his head back on the head-rest, covered his face with his head-cloth, and went to sleep.

Hamdan looked at him pityingly and murmured: "Poor chap! Sleep as much as you like now, but you're going to get a surprise when you wake up!"

* * *

It was true. There was a surprise waiting in the Eastern Province, unforeseen by Salman—and unforeseen by Hamdan as well. The locusts had with unexpected speed swarmed over the Province from the desert, and in the course of ten days had destroyed the crop even before it had ripened.

THE WOMEN'S BATHS

Ulfat al-Idlibi

OUR HOUSEHOLD WAS TROUBLED by an unusual problem: my grandmother, who had passed the age of seventy, insisted on taking a bath at the beginning of every month at the public baths, or market baths as she used to call them.

In my grandmother's opinion the market baths had a delicious ambience about them which we, who had never experienced it, could not appreciate.

For our part we were afraid that the old lady might slip on the wet floor of the baths—this has often happened to people who go there—and break her leg, as her seventy years had made her bones dry and stiff; or she might catch a severe chill coming outside from the warm air of the baths and contract a fatal illness as a result. But how could we convince this stubborn old lady of the cogency of these arguments?

It was quite out of the question that she should give up a custom to which she had adhered for seventy years, and she had done so without ever once having been stricken with the mishaps we feared. Grandmother had made up her mind that she would keep up this custom as long as she was able to walk on her own two feet, and her tenacity in clinging to her point of view only increased the more my mother tried to reason with her.

Yet Mother never tired of criticizing her mother-in-law, arguing with her and attempting to demonstrate the silliness of her views, even if only by implication. Whenever the subject of the public baths came up my mother proceeded to enumerate their shortcomings from the standpoints of health, of society, and even of economics.

The thing which really annoyed Mother was that my grandmother

19

monopolized our only maid from the early morning onward on the day she went to the baths. She would summon her to her room to help her sweep it and change the sheets and do up the bundles to take to the baths. Then she would set out with her and would not bring her back until around sunset, when our maid would be exhausted and hardly able to perform her routine chores.

In our house I was the observer of a relentless, even though hidden, struggle between mother-in-law and daughter-in-law: between my grandmother, who clung to her position in the household and was resolved under no circumstances to relinquish it, and my mother, who strove to take her place.

Although girls usually side with their mother, I had a strong feeling of sympathy for my grandmother: old age had caught up with her since her husband had died some time before and left her a widow, and little by little her authority in the home shrank as my mother's authority gradually extended. It is the law of life: one takes, then one hands over to another in one's turn. But that does not mean we obey the law readily and willingly.

I used to feel a certain prick of pain when I saw Grandmother retire alone to her room for long hours after being defeated in an argument with Mother. I would sometimes hear her talking bitterly to herself, or I would see her monotonously shaking her head in silence, as though she were rehearsing the book of her long life, reviewing the days of her past, when she was the unchallenged mistress of the house, with the last word. I would often see her vent the force of her resentment on her thousand-bead rosary as her nervous fingers told its beads and she repeated the prayer to herself:

"Oh merciful God, remove this affliction!"

And who could this "affliction" be but my mother?

Then little by little she would calm down and forget the cause of her anger. There is nothing like the invocation of God for purifying the soul and enabling it to bear the hardships of life.

One day when I saw my grandmother getting her things ready to go to the market baths I had the idea of accompanying her, thinking that perhaps I might uncover the secret which attracted her to them. When I expressed my wish to accompany her she was very pleased, but my mother did not like this sudden impulse at all, and said, in my grandmother's hearing, "Has the craze for going to the market baths affected you as well? Who knows—you may catch some infection, like scabies or something, and it will spread around the family."

Thereupon my father broke in with the final word: "What is the matter with you? Let her go with her grandmother. All of us went to the public baths when we were young and it never did any of us any harm."

My mother relapsed into a grudging silence, while my grandmother gave an exultant smile at this victory—my father rarely took her side against my mother.

Then Grandmother led me by the hand to the room where her massive trunk was kept. She produced the key from her pocket and opened the trunk in my presence—this was a great honor for me, for the venerable trunk had never before been opened in the presence of another person—and immediately there wafted out of it a strange yet familiar scent, a scent of age, a smell of the distant past, of years which have been folded up and stored away. Grandmother drew out of the depths of the trunk a bundle of red velvet, the corners of which were embroidered with pearls and sequins.

She opened it in front of me and handed me a wine-colored bath-wrap decorated with golden stars. I had never set eyes on a more beautiful robe. She also gave me a number of white towels decorated around the edges with silver thread, saying "All these are brand new; no one has ever used them. I have saved them from the time I was married. Now I'm giving them to you as a present, since you are going to the baths with me. Alas . . . poor me. Nobody goes with me now except the servants."

She gave a deep, heart-felt sigh. Then she called the servant to carry the bundle containing our clothes and towels, and the large bag which held the bowl, the soap, the comb, the sponge-bag, the loofah,* the soil of Aleppo,† and the henna which would transform my grandmother's white hair to jet black. She put on her shawl, and we made our way toward the baths, which were only a few paces from our house. Times without number I had read the words on the little plaque which crowned the low, unpretentious door as I passed by: "Whoever the Divine Blessing of health would achieve, should turn to the Lord and then to the baths of Afif."

We entered the baths.

The first thing I noticed was the female "intendant." She was a stout woman, sitting on the bench to the right of persons coming in. In front of her was a small box for collecting the day's revenue. Next to it was a *nargileh*‡ decorated with flowers. It had a long mouthpiece

---

*The fibrous pod of an Egyptian plant, used as a sponge. (tr)

† A kind of clay, found around Aleppo, which is mixed with perfume used in washing the hair. (tr)

‡ An eastern tobacco pipe in which the smoke passes through water before reaching the mouth. (tr)

which the intendant played with between her lips, while she looked at those around her with a proprietorial air. When she saw us she proceeded to welcome us without stirring from her place. Then she summoned Umm Abdu, the bath attendant. A woman hastened up and gave us a perfunctory welcome. She had pencilled eyebrows, eyes painted with *kohl*,* and was dressed very neatly. She had adorned her hair with two roses and a sprig of jasmine. She was very voluble, and was like a spinning-top, never motionless, and her feet in her Shabrawi clogs made a rhythmic clatter on the floor of the baths. Her function was that of hostess to the bathers. She came up to my grandmother and led her to a special bench resembling a bed. Our maid hastened to undo one of our bundles, drawing out a small prayer rug which she spread out on the bench. My grandmother sat down on it to get undressed.

I was fascinated by what I saw around me. In particular my attention was drawn to the spacious hall called *al-barani*.† In the center of it was a gushing fountain. Around the hall were narrow benches on which were spread brightly-colored rugs where the bathers laid their things. The walls were decorated with mirrors, yellowed and spotted with age, and panels on which were inscribed various maxims. On one of them I read, "Cleanliness is part of Faith."

My grandmother urged me to undress. I took off my clothes and wrapped myself in the wine-colored bath-wrap, but as I was not doing it properly Umm Abdu came and helped me. She secured it around my body and then drew the free end over my left shoulder, making it appear like an Indian sari.

Then she helped my grandmother down from her bench, and conducted us toward a small door which led into a dark corridor, calling out at the top of her voice, "Marwah! Come and look after the Bey's mother!"

With a sigh a shape suddenly materialized in the gloom in front of me: it was a grey-haired, emaciated woman of middle age with a face in which suffering had engraved deep furrows. She was naked except for a faded cloth which hung from her waist to her knees. She welcomed us in a nasal tone, prattling on although I could not catch a single syllable of what she was saying, thanks to the babble of discordant voices which filled my ears and the hot thick steam which obstructed my sight; and there was a smell which nearly made me faint, the like of which I had never encountered in my life before. I felt nauseous, and was almost

---

*A powder, usually of antimony, used in eastern countries to darken the eyelids. (tr)

† The outer hall of a public bath. (tr)

sick, leaning against the maid for support.

Nevertheless, in a few moments I grew accustomed to the odor and it no longer troubled me; my eyes, also, became accustomed to seeing through the steam.

We reached a small hall containing a large stone basin. A number of women circled around in it, chatting and washing at the same time. I asked my grandmother: "Why don't we join them?"

She replied: "This is the *wastani;** I have hired a cubicle in the *juwani.* † I am not accustomed to bathing with the herd."

I followed her through a small door to the *juwani,* and found myself looking with confused curiosity at the scene that presented itself. There was a large rectangular hall, at each corner of which stood a large basin of white marble. Women sat around each one, busily engrossed in washing, scrubbing, and rubbing, as though they were in some kind of race. I raised my eyes to look at the ceiling, and saw a lofty dome with circular openings, glazed with crystal, through which enough light filtered to illuminate the hall. The uproar here was at its worst—there was a clashing of cans, the splashing of water, and the clamor of children.

My grandmother paused for a moment to greet a friend among the bathers, while I found myself following a violent quarrel which had arisen between two young women. I understood from the women around them that they were two wives of a polygamous marriage, who had met face to face for the first time at the baths. The furious quarrel led at length to an exchange of blows with metal bowls. Luckily a spirit of chivalry among some of the bathers induced them to separate the two warring wives before they could satisfy their thirst for revenge.

As we advanced a little way the howling of a small child drowned the hubbub of the hall. Its mother had put it on her lap, twisting one of its legs around her and proceeding to scrub its face with soap and pour hot water over it until its skin was scarlet red. I averted my gaze, fearing the child would expire before my eyes.

We reached the cubicle, and I felt a sense of oppression as we entered it. It consisted of nothing but a small chamber with a basin in the front. Its one advantage was that it screened those taking a bath inside from the other women.

We were received in the cubicle by a dark, stout woman with a pockmarked face and a harsh voice. The was Mistress Umm Mahmud. She took my grandmother from the attendant Marwah, who was being assailed by shouts from every direction:

---

*The middle hall of a public bath. (tr)
† The inner hall of a public bath. (tr)

"Cold water, Marwah, cold water, Marwah!"

The poor woman set about complying with the bathers' requests for cold water, dispensing it from two big buckets which she filled from the fountain in the outer hall. She was so weighed down with the buckets that she aroused pity in those who saw her struggle.

I turned back to Grandmother and found her sitting on the tiled floor in front of the basin. She had rested her head between the hands of Umm Mahmud, who sat behind her on a sort of wooden chair which was only slightly raised above the level of the floor. She proceeded to scour Grandmother's head with soap seven consecutive times—not more, not less.

I stood at the door of the cubicle, entertained by the scene presented by the bathers. I watched the younger women coming and going, from time to time going into the outer hall for the sake of diversion, their fresh youthfulness showing in their proud swaying gait. In their brightly colored wraps decorated with silver thread they resembled Hindu women in a temple filled with the fragrance of incense. Little circles of light fell from the dome onto their tender-skinned bodies, causing them to glisten.

I found the sight of the older women depressing: they sat close to the walls chatting with one another, while the cream of henna on their hair trickled in black rivulets along the wrinkles of their foreheads and cheeks, as they waited impatiently for their turn to bath.

Suddenly I heard shrill exclamations of pleasure. I turned toward their source, and saw a group of women gathered around a pretty young girl, loudly expressing their delight at some matter.

Mistress Umm Mahmud said to me: "Our baths are doing well today: we have a bride here, we have a woman who has recently had a child, and we have the mother of the Bey—may God spare her for us!"

It was no wonder that my grandmother swelled with pride at being mentioned in the same breath with a bride and a young mother.

I enjoyed standing at the door of the cubicle watching the bride and her companions. Then I caught sight of a fair well-built woman enveloped in a dark blue wrap, giving vent to overflowing joy with little shrieks of delight. I realized from the words she was singing that she must be the bride's mother:

"Seven bundles I packed for thee, and the eighth in the
    chest is stored;
To Thee, Whom all creatures need, praise be, oh
    Lord!"

A young woman, a relative or friend of the bride, replied:

"Oh maiden coming from the *wastani,* with thy towel all
scented,
He who at thy wedding shows no joy, shall die an infidel,
from Paradise prevented!"

The bride's mother continued the song:

"The little birds chirp and flutter among the trellis'd leaves;
How sweet the bride! The bath upon her brow now pearly
crowns of moisture weaves.
Thou canst touch the City Gate with thy little finger tip,
though it is so high;
I have waited long, long years for this day's coming nigh!"

But the best verse was reserved for the bridegroom's mother:

"Oh my daughter-in-law! I take thee as my daughter!
The daughters of Syria are many, but my heart only desires
and wishes for thee!
Pistachios, hazels and dates: the heart of the envious has
been sore wounded;
Today we are merry, but the envious no merriment shall
see!"

The singing finished as the bride and her companions formed a circle around a tray upon which had been placed cakes of Damascene
mincemeat, and a second one filled with various kinds of fruit. The
bride's mother busied herself distributing the cakes right and left, and
one of them fell to my share also!

In a far corner a woman was sitting with her four children around a
large dish piled with *mujaddarah** and pickled turnips, their preoccu-
pation with their meal rendering them completely oblivious to what was
going on around them in the baths. When the dish had been emptied of
food the mother took from a basket by her side a large cabbage. Grip-
ping its long green leaves, she raised it up and then brought it down hard
on the tiled floor, until it split apart and scattered into fragments. The
children tumbled over each other to snatch them up and greedily
devoured them, savoring their fresh taste.

Then my attention was diverted by a pretty girl, about fifteen or six-
teen years old, sitting on a bench along the wall of the boiler-house. She
seemed impatient and restless, as though she found it hard to tolerate
the pervasive heat. She was surrounded by three women, one of whom,
apparently her mother, was feverishly fussing over her. She began to
rub over her body a yellow ointment which exuded a scent of ginger (it

*A Syrian dish of rice, lentils, onions, and oil. (tr)

was what was called "strengthening ointment"). My grandmother explained to me that it reinforced the blood vessels of a new mother, and restored her to the state of health she had enjoyed before having her child.

The attendant Umm Abdu came up to us and inquired after our comfort. She brought us both glasses of licorice sherbet as a present from the intendant. Then she lit a cigarette for my grandmother, who was obviously regarded as a patron of distinction.

It was now my turn. My grandmother moved aside, and I sat down in her place, entrusting my head to the attentions of Umm Mahmud for a thorough rubbing. After I had had my seven soapings I sat down before the door of the cubicle to relax a little. I was amused to watch the bath attendant Marwah scrubbing one of the bathers. Her right hand was covered with coarse sacking, which she rubbed over the body of the woman sitting in front of her. She began quite slowly, and then sped up, and as she did so little grey wicks began to appear under the sacking, which quickly became bigger and were shaken to the floor.

After we had finished being loofah-ed and rubbed, Umm Mahmud asked me to come back to her to have my head soaped an additional five times. I surrendered to her because I had promised myself that I would carry out the bathing rites through all their stages and degrees as protocol dictated, whatever rigors I had to endure in the process!

I was not finished until Umm Mahmud had poured the last basinful of water over my head, after anointing it with "soil of Aleppo," the scent of which clung to my hair for days afterwards.

Umm Mahmud rose, and standing at the door of the cubicle, called out in her harsh voice: "Marwah! Towels for the Bey's mother!"

With a light and agile bound Marwah was at the door of the *wastani,* calling out in a high-pitched tone, like a cockerel: "Umm Abdu! Towels for the Bey's mother!" Her shout mingled with that of another "Mistress" who was standing in front of a cubicle opposite ours, likewise demanding towels for her client.

Umm Abdu appeared, clattering along in her Shabrawi clogs, with a pile of towels on her arm which she distributed among us, saying as she did: "Blessings upon you . . . Have an enjoyable bath, if God wills!"

Then she took my grandmother by the arm and led her to the *barani,* where she helped her to get up onto the high bench, and then to dry herself and get into her clothes.

Grandmother stood waiting her turn to pay her bill. There was a heated argument going on between the intendant and a middle-aged woman who had three girls with her. I gathered from what was being said that the usual custom was for the intendant to charge married women in full, but that widows and single women paid only half the normal fee. The lady was claiming that she was a widow, and her daughters were all single. The intendant listened to her skeptically, and obviously could not believe that the eldest of the girls was single, in that she was an adult and was very beautiful. But at last she was forced to accept what the woman said after the latter had sworn the most solemn oath that what she was saying was the truth.

My grandmother stepped forward and pressed something into the intendant's hand, telling her: "Here's what I owe you, with something extra for the cold water and the attendance."

The intendant peered down at her hand and then smiled; in fact she seemed very pleased, for I heard her say to my grandmother: "May God keep you, Madam, and we hope to see you every month."

Then my grandmother distributed tips to the attendant, the "Mistress," and Marwah, as they emerged from the *juwani* to bid her good-bye.

I have never known my grandmother to be so generous and open-handed as on the day which we spent at the market baths. She was pleased and proud as she listened to the blessings called down on her by those who had received her largesse. Then she gave me an intentionally lofty look, as if to say: "Can you appreciate your grandmother's status now? How about telling your mother about *this*, now that she's begun to look down her nose at me?"

As she left the baths there was a certain air of haughtiness in her step, and she held herself proudly upright, although I had only known her walk resignedly, with a bent back, at home.

Now she was enjoying the esteem which was hers only when she visited the market baths. At last I understood their secret . . .

THE ANTS AND THE QAT

Haydar Haydar

AS THE FIRST ANT CRAWLED over the toe of Mahmud ibn Abdullah al-Zubayri as he lay beneath the tree, he gazed at it for a moment; an idle chuckle overcame him as he watched the diminutive creature climb over his giant body. In a sweetly languorous state he chewed a mouthful of qat,* moving it about in his mouth with relish, like a man caressing a woman's breast.

Mahmud ibn Abdullah al-Zubayri said to himself: "What a pity these poor mites are deprived of this pleasure!"

The sunlight, piercing through the leaves of the tree, combined with the delicious taste of the qat to produce a refreshing torpor in the body of the man, lying half in the sun and half in the shade. From a nearby café wafted the voice of an eastern singer, bearing him away to an ineffable tranquility.

Just as he was sucking the morsel of qat and greedily squeezing the last drop from it, another ant, followed by a companion, began to scale the toes of his supine body. The ascent of the third ant tickled him. Then the ant nipped him with its tiny jaws, and it felt as though a small thorn had pricked him. Mahmud ibn Abdullah said, "How stupid ants are!" and with a drowsy movement stirred his toes to shake the ant off or crush it. The ant, however, was more deft than this movement: it abandoned his toe and descended to the sole of his foot.

Torpor oozed into every cell of the man's recumbent body. He gave himself up to the sun, the qat, and the sweet soothing voice of the Star

---

*A shrub native to Arabia, the leaves of which are chewed to produce a pleasant state of drugged elation. (tr)

28

of the East.* The sleepy daze gave rise to visions and variegated day-dreams, like a rainbow. He saw himself flying above the fields and mountains until he had reached the stars in their courses. As he looked on the stars they changed to flowers. He plucked them and put them in his buttonhole, proudly displaying himself like a peacock. Then he noticed that the stars had been transformed into golden globes. He took them to sell in the market place, and with the money bought guns and horses and falcons and hunting dogs.

When he was weary of the stars and the gold and the guns and the falcons, he dreamed of white-skinned women the color of snow, their hair like ears of corn, and their eyes the color of the sea.

Then he imagined himself a knight riding into the wind, with a sword and a lance in his hand, and he was the unchallenged monarch of the world; and lo! Here was the world at his feet, with him issuing commands as he pleased, while around him serfs, slave-girls and soldiers obeyed his every whim. He married several wives, and allotted a palace and a night to each one.

At length, when his rule was firmly established, he considered it a good idea to eliminate his enemies—beginning with his neighbor of long standing, she of the sharp tongue, whom he had desired, but who had rebuffed him. He summoned her and condemned her, ordering her to kneel naked at his feet and to acknowledge that he was a king without peer in manliness and courage. Then he ordered his executioner to cut out her tongue, and passed her over to his slaves, for each of them to have, one after the other.

The happy king Mahmud ibn Abdullah al-Zubayri then commanded that a certain man should be brought to him who had once comprehensively described him as impotent, an ignoramus and a fool. He ordered his two hangmen to flog him until the blood flowed. Then they emasculated him and threw the remains to the dogs in front of the assembled people.

Then Mahmud ibn Abdullah al-Zubayri, recumbent upon his throne, began to avenge himself upon his enemies one after another, while the tiny insignificant ants climbed over the body swimming in its dreamy stupor. Now they were slowly making their way in throngs over it, attacking it with confidence.

The man's eyelids began to grow heavy; the visions and the fantasies began to dance, and jump from mountaintop to mountaintop, from city to city, as he was borne aloft on a gentle breeze and one imaginary voice melted into another, from star to star, from the sweet-

*Umm Kulthum, the famous Arab woman singer. (tr)

voiced eastern songstress. The overpowering qat coursed through his thirsty veins.

Mahmud ibn Abdullah al-Zubayri slept as the sun began to decline toward the horizon. Deep sleep carried him to remote islands filled with mermaids and buried treasures: treasures of rubies, diamonds and qat. Then he noticed that all these islands with all their treasures and rocks and trees had become a forest of qat trees. He embraced it with open arms and went on chewing with savage ecstasy.

The ants had now become armies. They swarmed from all directions, invading the body of the dreaming man; they pried all over him without let or hindrance. When the ants with their formic instinct had made sure that the man was beyond the sphere of consciousness and that the chewing had ceased, they peered at the fixed wide stupid smile, and began their relentless work on their prey, which had now become transformed into a corpse.

ANOTHER HARD WINTER

Sa'id Huraniyyah

My God, how long the night of darkness, how hard its winter!

Heinrich Heine

I HAD A SINGULAR AFFECTION for the graceful lemon tree which grew in our garden; I do not think I have ever had such a firm devotion to any other thing. The tree resembled one of the elegant princesses of whom I have read in story books, a real Damascene princess, sitting on her couch dressed in green silk, with her windows open to the green hills, and the book between her slender fingers adorned with threads of green brocade. She would sway to and fro, and then would stay motionless, completely composed, pearls sparkling from the tips of her fingers.

She was too prudent to philosophize; she simply passed her life in the enjoyment of beauty, and her handmaidens would come and go softly so that no noise should disturb her, covering her with the fragrant perfume of lilies, enveloping her room in a shimmering cloud of rainbow hues. When they closed the windows at dewy nightfall, as the sad songs of the pine trees still mourned in the kingdom of darkness, they would leave the curtains raised—that she might continue her pondering and gazing at the stars.

She was a true princess indeed. My princess was frail. She shook beneath the gusts of the biting wind. Oh! This accursed ghoul that stripped her of her leaves and wildly snatched them away, leaving her green life-blood congealing on her branches like tears of crystal.

He went about his business like a barbarian lover, stripping his loved one by tearing off her clothes piece by piece. His icy fingers with

31

their sharpened nails scratched her and sought to penetrate her with greedy lust; she shuddered, but she resisted bravely. Did I not say she was a true princess?

I began to observe her closely as she was putting forth her first blossoms, like some sweet mother. It is true that she began to look dumpy with the effects of her pregnancy; yet her leaves still fluttered skittishly in their proud, lustrous green. I delight in greenness. Would the good Lord have annoyed many people if he had created the sky green for my sake? It was morning, and the blossoms had contracted to little round spheres—the ground beneath the beautiful mother was covered with the remains of her flowers, which had died to bestow life.

That morning my father gave a little smile, and looked at us with composure. Then he shook his head. Deep inside I was exultant, because my father had always looked down upon the lemon tree, referring to her as "the spoilt child," observing her growth and struggle upward toward the sun with an indifference which cut one to the quick. I did not understand Father. Why did he not love my beautiful princess? Was it possible that anyone who had seen her waving tresses, the burnished green of her leaves, and her flowers dripping with honey should not fall in love with her till his dying day?

Father would say: "Lemon trees are weak and soft and have no resistance against storms. It only needs a light gust of wind to make them shake to their roots. This one is sick—like a consumptive—she always needs someone to help her and prop her up. If her trunk were to be slightly grazed her life would drain away drop by drop—she would never think of braving the pain and treating the scratch so as to get better. She stands there as though a great thunderbolt were about to fall upon her and make all her trembling leaves flap like the ears of a cringing donkey; and when she does produce lemons, she cannot hold onto them—even her own children dislike her. When she does die her wood will quickly flare up and burn to nothing, like a whore. Let me tell you the truth of it, children: I do not trust lemon trees at all. Much better to look at the oak trees. What strength and what endurance!"

Tears glistened in my eyes as I listened to Father belittling my princess and dragging her in the gutter. I abandoned the respectful manners due from a child to its parent and burst out: "The oak? you can love that decrepit old thing which lords it over the garden as much as you like. It's like a barren old hag, hard and cruel. May I be struck down if I ever give it another drop of water! All its life it has been a nuisance: it stuck its thorns* into us and stung our faces with its branches without mercy.

---

*The variety of oak referred to in this story is the holm oak. (tr)

It's so stupid and lacking in feeling that however many times I have carved my name on it, it has never let out so much as a moan!

"Anyone can belittle princesses, without giving them a chance to defend themselves. You have given her a whipping knowing that she cannot get her own back . . . it's a shame!"

I turned away from him in a flood of tears without giving him time to reply, taken aback as he was, and I locked the door of my room in his face, giving no answer to his repeated knockings.

Feeling lonely, I thought: "The oak tree and Father are so alike!— His wrinkled face, his deep-set eyes, brooding coldly over the affairs of the world, his astonishing fortitude with the ups and downs of life, without one seeing the least sign on his face of what is going on inside him, his hatred of weakness and crying, his steady persistence in promptly putting to right things that have gone awry!"

As I pondered this it seemed to me that he was a chip off the oak tree. "And why not? Didn't Mother once tell me that she had found me in the branches of the vine which clings to the wall of our house; the vine whose clusters of grapes are constantly stung by hornets intent on shedding its blood? It is a pity I did not ask my grandmother before she died about the place where she found my father when he was little; it must have been somewhere in the oak tree. He only hates my princess because she is tender and soft and fruitful."

At that instant my cat jumped from her place on the bed and stood in front of me twitching her tail, arching her back and yawning. Then she curled up on my lap, letting my hand glide through her fur as she closed her eyes and purred with contentment.

Why doesn't Father play with us? It's true he loves us and is kind to us, but he has never stroked my hair or caressed my shoulder as I am doing with the cat . . . the only thing he ever does is to frown severely whenever any one of us cries. He has always detested tears: as though children were grown-up men. He always says: "You must not cry. A time is coming when nobody will be surprised at children's tears. But at this moment it is something to be ashamed of. You must learn to bear things with fortitude."

And when Mother died, and we filled the whole house with weeping and wailing, he sat silent in his room, his troubled eyes staring into space, shedding not a single tear. Had he not really loved my mother? It is true he did not remarry, and continued to revere her memory, but I could never forgive him his coldness . . . only last week he rebuked my brother Adil when a heavy piece of wood fell on his head and he cried out in pain. Father said to him severely: "You're a man now, and real men do not cry!" He did not address another word to him for two days. It almost made the poor fellow ill. Oh how I hate this oak tree!

* * *

When winter approached, the few remaining lemons on my princess hung in yellow, transparent beauty. At twilight I used to gaze at her as she joyfully danced in the moist breeze. The little princesses would exchange tender, spontaneous glances of love with the setting sun . . . The happy mother would smile gaily, and then, when she noticed that the sun had kindled a scorching warmth in the little hearts opened to the light, she would extend her moist, shining leaves and caress their soft cheeks tenderly. Then she would cover them from the eyes of the sun, which at times appeared more sinister than benevolent.

Father approached the princess and shook her gently, looking up at the clouds in the sky. Then he said meaningfully, as though talking to himself: "The winter's going to be hard this year, I think. I hope the lemon tree will be able to stand up to the frost when it comes into its first bearing. It looks as though it is about to fall down."

I felt his words plunge into my breast like a knife. My eyes filled with tears, but I tried to hide them from my father, who pretended to look the other way. Struggling to control myself, I said: "It's perfectly strong, Father. Just look at its leaves and see how fresh and green and attractive they are. Look at its vigorous roots and see how deeply they sink into the soil. See how its height increases day by day. It is a true princess, Father, and princesses do not give up easily."

Father replied firmly: "I have no confidence in her."

"But Father, she will put up resistance. She will resist and not let anything defeat her. She is beautiful and unapproachable: see how her eyelashes flutter reproachfully against you!"

Turning away, Father replied: "Give her support, my boy, if you wish. Tie one rope around the top of her trunk and one around the bottom and attach them to the wall, and stop watering her every day: it makes the soil friable and then it is easily washed away when we get a heavy downpour."

But then he repeated: "I have no confidence in her. I have no confidence in pampered pets who do not know how to look after their children."

When Father had gone I ran to the lemon tree to hug her, and said: "You will resist, won't you Princess? Prove that princesses can triumph over storms. Don't be misled by Father, my dear friend; he is kind really, despite his gruffness. If you hold out this year he will love you more than the oak tree, and I shall bring you a golden bird for a crown, and I shall make it sing to you all day."

The princess bent her boughs in an embrace and her leaves caressed my face.

As I walked away I prayed: "Oh Lord, look after my princess. You cannot let this grace and beauty perish. Mother said that you are Beauty and love beautiful things: then protect this beautiful thing for me!"

* * *

The raging wind, moaning eerily, began to lash our sitting-room windows. I drew the curtains back and stared out into the blackness of the night. The light from the room fell feebly onto my princess. My heart pounded . . . it was just as though a great strong giant had clasped her neck in his powerful hands and was proceeding to shake her, to squeeze the life from her drop by drop. She was swaying and bending wildly, her fruits clinging desperately to the branches. Her leaves had begun to fly around and disappear into the darkness like flimsy black feathers. Her tender stem clung to the soil defiantly with slender fingers . . . my tears welled up and my love was overlaid with foreboding.

Father had the fire tongs in his hand and was taking pieces of glowing olive-wood from the stove and placing them in the brazier. The lines on his face deepened as he said: "I do not dislike the winter. In spite of everything it can do it is weak compared with One Who is stronger."

Carefully wrapping Father's coat around him, my brother said: "As far as I am concerned, I cannot stand it. Winter for me is a picture of specters leaving their abodes and snatching at people to terrify them— and then dragging them away to their noisome lairs. And then the people can only emerge into daylight again as craven, shifty goblins."

Father replied pensively: "Ghosts are pitiable creatures. They can only influence weak people, whose only power is that of pretence and deceit. A ghost is like a hyena which knows its man: if it senses courage and resolution it flees from him, but if it perceives that he is craven-hearted and lacks confidence in himself and his strength, it mesmerizes him and has its way with him."

I replied, fighting my depression: "It's a very severe winter. I wonder if my lemon tree will be able to put the ghosts to flight?"

Father, as though he had not heard me, said: "You don't yet understand anything of snow or rain or frost or wind. During the cold days you have always been within the four walls of this room, with a stove in front of you burning olive-wood, with deerskin sofas and wool rugs beneath your feet. I am very much afraid, children, that one day winter will catch you unawares, when you are outside the room, standing naked and cold before the blast; just like the oak tree outside in the garden. Then no one but God knows how you will fare."

Coaxingly I said: "And what about my princess, Father?"

He was silent for a moment, as his eyes seemed to be staring at something in the far distance, and then he went on, without answering my question: "When the snow falls in flakes the size of the palm of your hand . . ."

I drew the curtains a second time and great white flakes were filling the sky and dancing together in the gloom. My princess was completely covered in a flowing white robe. I exclaimed, interrupting my father: "It's been snowing, Father! There are great flakes the size of the palm of the hand. They've covered . . ." I choked out the words.

Father coughed, and murmured with a frown: "God's mercy be upon us. It's going to be another hard winter."

I looked at him hard . . . what a strange man he was. It was as though magic forces were at work deep within him. I shivered fearfully as I imagined the snow burying my princess and extinguishing the spark of life in her. How could Father sit there by his stove as though nothing in the world could disturb him, the fire tongs in his hand, busying himself with the stove with the deftness of a helmsman steering a ship? Today however he was doing this with a certain air of distraction. He asked me: "Did you say that the snowflakes are the size of the palm of one's hand?"

The fire had begun to penetrate the dry wood and encircle it; its bloodshot eyes reddened with passion as the wood crackled and the heart-wood opened. Suddenly the fire tongs slipped in Father's hand at the mouth of the stove and a red-hot cinder fell out onto the expensive carpet. My brother rushed to fetch the coal-shovel, but couldn't find it. Father tried to pick it up with the tongs, but it crumbled, and a pungent smell of burning filled the room. Father put out his hand and picked up a cinder with his fingers. We cried out in alarm: "Mind your hand, Father!"

But Father continued the operation quickly and with fortitude, rubbing his hand after picking up each cinder. Frightened by this exhibition I cried out: "Your hands are getting charred, Father: they're bleeding!"

He made no reply. He picked up all the pieces of cinder without so much as a twitch of his facial muscles. When he had finished he looked up at us, suppressing a wry smile, and said rather breathlessly: "Don't worry—if you play with fire you must put up with burned fingers."

He took out his handkerchief and held the palms of his hands open to bind up the burned spots. They were raw and stained with blood. I couldn't stand the sight—and fainted.

* * *

Oh God, how miserable I feel! My beautiful princess has died and has been buried without any ceremony or silken shroud. She lingered for a long time, but my fervent prayers did not help her to stay alive.

Her green leaves, after turning yellow, fell off one by one; her roots withered and appeared above the surface of the soil. Her yellow fruits, disfigured and split open, fell to the ground, where their blood flowed upon the earth, scattered and misshapen like miscarried embryos. My princess was left as naked as when God created her, shamefully bare, rigid like a bird surprised by a snake, a skeleton frozen by fright. A spider started to weave its web over her decayed remains. The perfidious birds no longer bestowed so much as a glance upon her.

Then one day Father took his axe to her. She snapped very easily, just like a piece of dry thorn-wood. As I watched I felt as though his axe were cutting through my veins; fiery tears of blood were flowing in my heart.

When he had finished his butchery he turned from her dead, mutilated remains and said to me consolingly: "Don't be sad, my boy. It was just one of the poor victims of the winter. I told you before that it was frail and extremely soft. I don't trust lemon trees."

I vented my anger on him: "But your great oak tree has died too! Haven't you noticed how its leaves have withered and fallen? I'll cut it down tomorrow just as you've cut down my princess."

Father replied with a certain acerbity: "Don't trouble yourself, my boy. Oak wood is hard to cut. You may hurt yourself."

"It's dead, and the Devil's taken its soul."

As Father went inside, cutting the argument short, a note of anxiety cracked through his voice, which he tried to hide: "It's accustomed to resisting the storms of winter. I think it will live. It's a sturdy oak."

I observed it day by day: there was no trace of life in its speckled trunk and its bare, scarred branches! But it always gave me an impression of grandeur. And one morning in spring I woke up early and ran out to it. I saw my father standing there looking as though he were a piece of it. I raised my glance to the branches and was thunderstruck. Oh this accursed hag in the guise of youth! She was like a cat with nine lives! For on every branch were tender green twigs covered with downy young leaves, trembling and drinking in the sunlight.

Father did not notice me. He began to pat its trunk with affection. Then he turned round to me, and it seemed to me that two tears the color of the oak tree started from his stern eyes. The furrows on his face quickly absorbed them, however, like thirsty land soaking up the rain.

WONDERING WHO ...

Walid Ikhlasi

I WAS CULLING THROUGH OLD PAPERS and various odds and ends which had accumulated in my desk and on my cupboard shelves. There were innumerable reasons that drove me to do this, but most important was that I wanted to make a fresh beginning. The sun was going down and the hours were waning like the walls of a decaying fortress. The room was small, and there was a noise at the window like that of a hungry cat.

If I had gone on as before I would have had hallucinations. I would have been driven to write mournful poetry; I should certainly have deteriorated into a state of permanent drowsiness, or . . .

Now I think to myself: "I certainly got rid of all those papers and odds and ends, and my boredom as well, while I was searching for a different, vital existence in the present. And what happened? I have landed in a terrible predicament, and I have no idea whether I shall be able to extricate myself from it, and go back to my old, ordinary existence."

I had paused to thumb through an old address book which I had once liked to keep by me. It had fallen among the torn-up scraps of paper, and I was surprised as I snatched it up and brushed the dust off it. It contained hundreds of addresses, names of friends, acquaintances and colleagues, notes and telephone numbers; addresses of people who had died and who had been crossed out; alterations and substitutions; addresses from all quarters of the globe, men and women, names which provoked memory upon memory—here a smile, there a passing twinge of pleasure, here a reminder of happiness, there a friend in the war.

Twilight fell and I was still reading it, as though it were a novel that was impossible to put down. Every address had a story attached to it, and it was not so easy to go back over my past life and at the same time seek something new and fresh; yet I felt the desire to recall everything connected with the people I had known. Memories unfolded themselves before me like the refrain of a song, repeated over and over again but to a different tune. Here was the address of a girl who once said to me: "I cannot find words to tell you how much I love you"—and then went off with someone else. Here was the address of an old school friend who said in the last letter I received from him a year ago, "Dear ——, I cannot stand it here any longer. I won't be coming back."

Here was an address with a frame of red ink around it, which must have once held considerable interest for me, unlike now, as I tried to skip over it—but without sufficient care to avoid recalling certain painful memories associated with it. Could I really be mesmerized by the mere name of a man who once humiliated me, whereupon I resolved upon revenge—but later forgot all about it? I tried to escape from the snare, but the past, beginning to stir from its slumber like an adder in the warmth of spring, slowly drew me toward it, as though I were impotent in its grasp.

The fellow shouted in my face. I shouted back blankly. He brandished the stick he held in all directions.

My brain worked like a computer, devising plans of revenge. His rancor-filled eyes seemed to twitch like the second-hand of a watch. I had to give way—my pulse felt as though it were in his grip. His stick pounded against my body. The weals overflowed with pain, as though sulfuric acid were boring into my bones. No . . . I no longer wished for vengeance; the painful memories began to fade as soon as I passed over this address framed in red ink, to the next one, which meant nothing to me.

I spent several minutes trying hard to remember something about this address, but without success. This undivided concentration was the only way to avoid the painful memories I had conjured up. I looked at the address this way and that, but it remained mute before me, a locked house of secrets. After a while I had completely forgotten the previous address, and was wrestling with this fresh puzzle.

Now I wish I had persisted with that red-framed conundrum, and had not started cudgeling my brains over this further mystifying address, like some busybody meddling with a hornet's nest.

But I felt I just had to remember something. The name meant nothing to me—Hikmat Ahmad Farid.* Who on earth could this Hikmat

---

*This Arabic name can be that of either a man or a woman. (tr)

be? His address indicated a nearby town easily reached by the main road. Perhaps he was an old school friend . . . no. Perhaps it was someone I had met on a journey . . . no. Could it be a pen pal? No. After casting around like this for some time I said to myself: "Why do I keep assuming that Hikmat is the name of a man, when it could just as well be the name of a woman?"

But who could this woman be? A girlfriend? No. A woman of easy virtue? No. A woman journalist? No. The representative of some firm, or the friend of a friend? No. My mind was a complete blank as far as this name was concerned, and I felt a sudden feeling of aversion for everything connected with it.

But after a while my curiosity grew, and I found myself longing to discover some details which would give definition to this shadowy being, be it man or woman. What was his or her age, profession, looks, social position? I wanted to know this mysterious being in the way that a playwright knows the composition of one of his characters. I tried and tried to fathom the nature of this wraith-like figure of the mysterious address, but without success. Dejection took possession of me once again, and this time I failed in the attempt to pass on to another address—or even to go back to the previous one.

Here and now I think: "If only I had put that address out of my head, and not gotten myself into this mess."

As I gulped down my fourth cup of coffee I thought to myself, deep down: "I cannot let this mystery go on haunting me. If I were really suffering from loss of memory, I should have forgotten everything—I should not even have recognized this address book and its contents. So why should it be just this particular name that I have forgotten? Why?"

A sense of weariness began to engulf me, when I was roused by a sudden thought—how would it be if I sent a letter to the unknown person, seeking his or her help?

I felt very happy when I had finished the letter, simply addressed to "Hikmat Ahmad Farid," without any "Mr." or "Mrs." or "Miss" added. I felt the pleasing anticipation of adventure each time I reread the letter to myself in my untidy room:

Dear Mr. or Dear Miss Hikmat Ahmad Farid,

This letter may arouse your curiosity, but my curiosity regarding *you* surpasses anything you can imagine. My interest in my address book, by which I set great store, has moved me to write to you, as I have tried hard to remember something, however small, about you and about why your name is in my address book, but without success.

The thing that really disturbs me is that I should come across a name in my address book which recalls no face at all and not a single memory. Knowledge of people and things is the basis of everything in life. For this reason I implore you to write to me the very minute you receive this letter, giving me any sort of reply you wish. Tell me how you came to know me. My happiness depends on your reply.

I shall be deeply disappointed if this request meets with your silence or delay.

To tell you the truth, at this moment I feel I could hate you, but if I receive a reply from you I shall love and respect you.

My address is on the envelope, and if you would like me to call, I shall make haste to do so.

With kind regards,

* * *

Awaiting the reply gave life an enjoyable sense of purpose. I finished cleaning out my room, and order and tidiness were restored. A day passed, which I spent listening to foreign broadcasts, and in spite of the violent confrontations among the peoples of the world, the mounting war casualties, the floods, the epidemics, my smile did not leave my face. I glanced at it furtively in the mirror. It looked bright and carefree.

I passed another day perusing a book dealing with the subject of oppression through the ages. At the end of each chapter I relished the thought that I had not been born into circumstances such as those, and looked around me to seek reassurance, as the light fell across books, furniture, shoes—and cockroaches, which I allowed to pass on their way unmolested. I felt quite relaxed.

On the same day I asked myself, as I glanced outside at the people who were visible in the street for a few moments, before giving way to others, like the days of the week—I asked myself: "What if I went to visit Mr. or Mrs. Hikmat in person?"

Perhaps it was the fact that I was not familiar with the town where this person lived which encouraged me to find out something about the surroundings in which he or she existed—this individual who had aroused both my curiosity and anxiety. Would he remember anything of our shared experiences of the past? Would he greet me as eagerly as I would him? Could this person possibly be a beautiful woman who would radiate warmth and intimacy?

Again and again I asked myself, on that terrible day: "What if it really is a girl I once loved, and I find her married, living in a cozy little nest with no place in it for me? But perhaps it will turn out to be a man with whom I have nothing in common, and we shall disagree on everything and part as enemies."

I knew I should not be able to think of anything else until I could visualize the missing face, and I fell into a doze until the postman should knock at the door bringing welcome news.

Now I think to myself: "How I wish I had sunk into a deep sleep, and not woken up at all when the knocks came at the door"—which I had opened as an undefined sense of foreboding came over me.

The knock at the door was repeated—and then it seemed as though more than one person were knocking. I picked myself up from my sprawled position on the comfortable sofa and made for the door. It was as though I were still dreaming. A much louder knocking came from the door. I opened it—and my astonishment burgeoned in the space between me and five pairs of eyes which met my gaze.

"Is Mr. —— here," asked a burly man dressed in ordinary, commonplace clothes. I replied with a politeness which sprang from my astonishment. "*I* am Mr.——. What can I do for you, gentlemen?"

"You may put the rest of your things on and then come with us."

Another man, who was smoking, added, "I'll just step inside with you, if you don't mind."

I thought: "There must be some mistake: this is the way they treat a criminal suspect." Aloud, I said: "All right, you may all come in."

A few minutes later we were in a car—I knew when we drew up at a big doorway that it was an official car—but I did not query it, or ask why I should be in it, nor did I question the big entrance hall, from which we proceeded to a long corridor leading to a low-ceilinged room, which would hardly admit anybody of average size. Here there were three doors facing us. One of these was something like the door of a big refrigerator. A short man opened it and I was the first one to step inside. The place was freezing cold. In the middle of the room was a longish table with a bundled shape on it which looked like somebody sleeping. One of the men who stood around me in a half-circle took off the white sheet, and said in a formal tone which reminded me of my old mathematics teacher:

"Do you know this woman?"

My sole feeling at that moment was one of frightened disgust—it was the face of a brunette, covered in congealed blood, which had stuck her hair to her scalp. Her look of horror corresponded to mine. It was the first time I had seen the corpse of someone who had been killed in violent fashion.

"Do you know this woman?"

I gazed at the glazed eyes which were like the blood of a deep wound, and said in a low voice: "How ghastly! How was she killed?"

"Do you know this woman?"

"No."

After a few moments the voice penetrated for the third time the wall of horror between by ear and the speaker: "Do you deny that you knew this woman?"

As I visualized the woman as she must have appeared in life, and tried to imagine the laugh which had faded away at the corners of her mouth as it had tightened under the stress of sudden terror, I said calmly: "I don't deny anything, gentlemen; I know nothing whatever about it."

I heard one of them whisper (in spite of his obvious wish not to be overheard): "Let's take him back to the Chief."

Although none of them were listening, I objected: "I suppose I'm to be a prosecution witness for a crime of which I know nothing!"

As I got back into the car, accompanying the men to the next unknown destination, I mentally concentrated on the dead woman, posing questions to her about her headstrong youth, leading her to a cold slab in a mortuary. But the image printed on my eyes left no room for her to return an answer. Somebody must now be mourning for her. I felt like asking one of the men escorting me, but they simply looked straight ahead, not listening, and I said nothing.

The Chief, with whom I was left alone in a cheerless room, was a man with motionless eyes. He went on reading the documents scattered in front of him. Then, as though he had just returned to consciousness after a deep sleep, he rapped out: "You know the penalty for murder?"

"Death, of course."

He shouted at me again—and it was clear that he was a man who conserved his energies for occasions of pleasure, or as now, of stress: "Good. We begin sensibly. It appears that you are not going to make me lose my patience."

"Who said I wanted to make anyone lose their patience?"

"Then what caused you to deny that you knew the woman?"

"What woman?"

"The murdered woman!"

"The murdered woman?"

He replied coldly, as though he were merely part of the office equipment: "Are you starting to deny it again? Here is a woman who has died as the result of a criminal assault committed by a certain man; we have the identity of this man and all he has to do is confess."

I was on the point of letting out a sharp exclamation of annoyance, but managed to control myself: "It's no concern of mine whether he confesses or not. The point is I don't know what you're talking about."

At this he pulled out a picture of a woman from a drawer. "Do you know this woman?"

I looked hard at it and then said triumphantly: "It's the murdered woman. I recognize her from—"

But before I could finish he shouted: "Then you do recognize her!"

"I saw her in the mortuary!"

At this point it was apparent that his limited stock of patience was running out. He shouted: "Do you know a person by the name of Hikmat Ahmad Farid?"

I replied heatedly, with a voice that reverberated around the room: "I only wish I did know her!"

He retorted coldly: "Don't treat me like a fool. This picture is of Hikmat Ahmad Farid."

Staring hard at the picture which he held out close to my face I shouted in panic: "But I don't recognize her!"

Was it conceivable that she had been that unresponsive corpse? Was it conceivable that this was the person about whom I had been asking myself question after question?

The Chief was reading from a paper, which I knew was my letter: "To tell you the truth, at this moment I feel I could hate you . . ." He looked at me sternly. "Who wrote these words? Are you trying to tell me I wrote them?"

"No, I wrote them."

"Then how can you keep insisting you don't know the murdered woman, Hikmat Ahmad Farid? A confession would reduce your sentence."

There was a pause. Then he picked up a large card from among the papers and began reading from it in a monotone:

"Hikmat Ahmad Farid, 22 years of age. Parents both dead. Had two or possibly three abortions. Father unknown. Unmarried according to official records. Courted by numerous men. Poems composed in her honor. Worked as a model for a crippled artist, and as a reporter for press and radio. Killed with a sharp instrument which penetrated the cerebellum."

Waves of confusion passed over me as he looked up at me inquiringly, awaiting more details. With a weary air he said: "Your letter was a prominent item among her few belongings."

In a low voice, which the other man overheard, I breathed: "Luck was against me."

He retorted sharply: "Luck was against you because you overlooked the piece of evidence found in the room where the crime was committed."

The man was obviously not going to let me leave this place.

I said: "It's a long story. If only you would let me explain."

He cut me short. "If only you will have the goodness to make a confession—we have a lot of other cases demanding attention."

A few days later I was obliged to try to prove to them where I had been at the time the woman was murdered, and to think of one single thing that would justify my curiosity in investigating the name written in the address book. I had to justify the presence of that name in the book as well.

This morning I said to the Chief: "I'm innocent. I swear it."

"All of them swear, but we rarely believe them."

With his eyes fixed on the floor he continued: "What is your final wish?"

I took a grip on myself, bringing out the words calmly: "Is it true what the experts say about split personality? That one can have two, three, four personalities? My wish, gentlemen, is that I should be reprieved long enough to learn something about this matter."

But they have rejected my request.

SARAB*

Colette Khuri

SHE WAS STILL WAITING for him. She passed among people, oblivious to their presence.

A whole year had passed . . . and she was still waiting for him.

He had promised her he would come back and she had believed him . . . she believed him although she had only seen him once in her life—a whole year ago, on New Year's Eve.

With him she had said farewell to a whole year of long days, and welcomed a year of long nights . . . and she was still waiting!

She glanced at her small wristwatch. It was eight o'clock.

When she had met him last year it had been at eight o'clock.

He was a man fleeing from the nightmare of the past.

A chance meeting had brought them together on New Year's Eve. Their eyes had met . . . and in their meeting desolation had vanished. Hope had burgeoned in the brightness of their eyes. She had smiled . . . and he had spoken. She still remembered the tone of his strong voice: "Let's forget the questions . . . let's bury our memories . . . we have both lost the past. Let's search for the future together."

Reserve had melted in the warmth of two hands intertwined.

The rain was pouring down. Sarab pulled up the collar of her raincoat. She hid her hands in the big pockets and quickened her step, paying no attention to the thirsty eyes staring at her good looks. It had not been merely her good looks which had attracted him. Out of millions of men, he was the one with whom she had spent an evening.

A man about whom she knew absolutely nothing at all. She was

---

*The proper noun "Sarab" also means "mirage" in Arabic. (tr)

46

content to immerse herself in his depths, and refrained from asking him about his life. She did not know where he came from, nor did she ask him where he was going, but he promised her, when they parted at dawn, that he would return. And so she clung to the memory, and the days of a whole year had been submerged in one unforgettable evening. And she was still waiting for him.

Al-Salihiyya Street was crammed with people. It was the end of another year to which the Damascenes were hastening to bid farewell—another year just beginning which happy people were welcoming with smiles. The pearly lights of the cabarets glittered. The restaurants bade welcome to those with well-lined pockets. The tramps stretched themselves out on the pavement.

While she . . . she would spend the evening at the cinema. At the end of the performance she would go on to the little restaurant. The restaurant she had become acquainted with a year ago.

She would see the face of the absent one in the wine glass. The proprietor would come up to her to ask her as usual about the one who had not yet returned, and she would tell him: she was still waiting!

The rain poured down . . .

Sarab entered the foyer of the cinema. The next performance would begin in an hour. She would while away the time in the small lounge.

She sat down in a corner by herself and asked the waiter to bring a cup of coffee. Her glance moved among the people in the lounge. Suddenly—

Her eyes fastened on a man busy reading a magazine. She stared at him in astonishment and took a deep breath.

It was the one she was waiting for! It was for certain.

A tremor passed through her. Her face shone. She got up, went over to him and stood in front of him. Her tongue was tied with suspense. With an effort she said: "Good evening."

The man raised his head from his magazine and looked at her in surprise. Then he replied politely: "Good evening."

Ignoring his cool tone, she asked eagerly: "When did you arrive?"

The man looked surprised and stood up, replying: "Arrive? I arrived this evening."

The tone of indifference in his voice frightened her; she asked fearfully: "Have you forgotten me?"

Confused, he replied: "I beg your pardon . . ." He looked at her searchingly; then shook his head. "I'm sorry . . . have we met somewhere before?" He went on as he pulled up a chair. "Will you sit down, Miss . . .?"

She completed his sentence in a withdrawn tone: "Of course,

you've forgotten my name as well—Sarab. My name is Sarab." Disappointment numbed her apprehension. She sat down feeling suddenly tired. "Then . . . you don't remember . . ."

The man's perplexity increased: "Do you know *my* name?"

With forbearance she muttered: "Karam." Her voice sank to a whisper. "Karam . . . a sound that has been a song in my heart for a whole year."

His eyes opened wide: "Yes . . . that's my name . . . but no one calls me by it except my mother. My ordinary name is Abdul—Abdu 'l-Karim . . ."

For a long moment he stared hard at her. In vain he searched his memory to try to find this pretty face.

"Did . . . did we meet somewhere in Beirut?"

Tears glistened in her eyes: "No . . . we met here."

He gaped. "This is the first time in my life I have been to Damascus, Miss . . ."

Sarab insisted: "But we spent the evening together, on New Year's Eve."

"Spent the evening together in Damascus?"

His question swam in the depth of her wide-open eyes, and he smiled: "I expect you have made a mistake, Miss . . . I could never have forgotten an evening spent in the light of two such charming eyes. But I am not acquainted with Damascus. I do assure you: this is the very first time I have come to Damascus."

Sarab was silent. He continued: "But I am very happy . . ."

She interrupted him: "Don't you remember the small restaurant . . . 'The Candles Restaurant'?"

"But I assure you I do not know Damascus."

She tried again, despairingly: "We spent an evening there together . . ."

He took a grip on himself. "Are you quite sure that this man who spent the evening with you was me?"

After a long distracted moment she whispered: "Yes . . . we sat in the corner . . . in candlelight . . . the proprietor spoke with us for a while. We stayed up till dawn. We forgot the past and the future. You promised me you would return—and I have waited for you."

Baffled, the man asked: "But when was all this?"

"Last New Year's Eve."

He blurted out: "Last New Year's Eve? That's impossible, Miss . . . last New Year's Eve I was unconscious in Beirut University Hospital. I was under anaesthetics for a whole day . . ."

She felt giddy. She closed her eyes. What was the point of arguing?

He didn't remember a thing. Distress tore at her heart.

With a great effort she tried to hide the disappointment which almost erupted from her features. She stretched out her hand to the forgotten cup of coffee which the waiter had brought. She buried her distress in the dark liquid.

The man was moved by her obvious emotion and whispered: "Miss Sarab . . . I beg you . . . earnestly—don't be upset. I assure you I have seen you in my dreams—you are any man's dream. Don't be upset. I am a stranger here—a stranger altogether. Why not let's spend the evening together—why not let's welcome the New Year together?"

She turned her moist eyes to him: "No!"

She would not spend an evening with the hero of a tragedy in which she had played no role. But she would not reproach him. She took control of herself and muttered: "I will see . . . I must be going home now. I must . . . I'll get in touch with you in an hour."

"Please do. I'm staying at the 'Orient Palace.' "

"Goodbye."

He corrected her: "Au revoir!"

She took her departure. His eyes followed her form. Suddenly he felt a sense of emptiness: an emptiness unlike any emptiness he had ever felt before—a yawning emptiness circumscribed by her absence.

Then the realization came over him that this girl who had come from he knew not where was the missing link he had searched for all his life. Immediately he returned to the hotel and waited. Hours passed and no inquiry for him came from Sarab. He decided to search for her. She had told him about the little restaurant—the "Candles." He would go there. He might trace her there. He asked the hotel manager about the location of the restaurant, and set out to find it.

He stood by the entrance, feeling a perfect stranger. He peered around, looking for a half-forgotten picture of dancers in the candle-light. Someone he did not know approached him—perhaps it was the proprietor. He welcomed him: "Good evening, good evening . . . when did you arrive?"

The man cried out: "Arrive? I arrived this evening!" The proprietor went on: "Welcome, welcome . . . we are so glad that you've returned safely. Make yourself comfortable, Mr. Karam. It's been a long year. Haven't you met Miss Sarab yet?" Seeing the man's bewilderment, he added with a smile: "Never fear. She is quite well. And she is still waiting for you!"

THE DESTROYER OF FAMILIES

Sabah Muyhi 'l-Din

IN ALEPPO THERE IS AN OLD MARKET known as "The Medina."*
It is a town in itself, which people enter by a great gateway opposite the
ancient citadel of Aleppo. The visitor finds himself in a sort of tunnel,
to which light penetrates through openings in its high, domed roof. As
his eyes become accustomed to the prevailing semi-darkness, he
becomes aware that he is surrounded on all sides by little narrow shops,
resembling lamps set in a rock face. On platforms in front of the shops
sit the craftsmen and merchants, each engaged in the craft or trade
peculiar to that section of the market.

Every part has its own colors and smells and sounds: the market of
the perfumers with its fragrant scents of rose and jasmine and musk and
perfumed powders; the market of the shoemakers with its clusters of red
and yellow and white shoes dangling in front of its shops; the market of
the butchers with its pungent smell and its carcasses hung up by their
hamstrings and its aroma of roasting meat; the women's market with its
illuminated glass-fronted shops, with their gleaming earrings, finger-
rings and necklaces, in front of which women cluster, clucking like hens
crowding around grains of wheat on the threshing floor . . . and there are
many others.

Ever since I was a child I have loved wandering around them, getting lost (or losing myself), and savoring the pleasure of adventure and
exploration. I like to emerge finally in front of the Great Mosque, and
go in to sit down in the shade of one of its great wide colonnades, where
I linger and watch the ancient clock measuring the seconds and minutes

---

*Literally, "the town." (tr)

and indicating the phases of the moon and the positions of the stars.

Between the market of the perfumers and the women's market there is a short passage lined with shops darker than the rest. They have old, dusty glass fronts, through which one can spy—with difficulty—a strange medley of perfume bottles, *nargileh*s, rings, printed and manuscript books, Hittite figurines, African and Roman coins and pieces of carved woodwork, all jumbled together as though Time in its rapid course had flung them aside into this corner of the old market and forgotten them, like pieces of wreckage at the bottom of the sea.

I used to pass by these shops and spend a long time standing in front of them, fascinated by the objects in their windows, and picturing to myself their long and checkered histories. Legends and images of the past would fill my mind, evoked by these relics of bygone ages.

But I would never have thought of going into one of these shops—had it not been for my friend and contemporary at school, Kamal, the son of al-Hajj* Abdullah. Al-Hajj Abdullah used to squat in one of these shops and pose as the chief of the whole market, since he had been there longer than anyone else, and was keener than any of them in buying and selling—especially selling. As well as being concerned with "antiques," as he called them, he was very fond of traditional stories, being addicted to the "Thousand and One Nights," "The Story of Sayf son of Dhu Yazan," "Hamzat al-Bahlawan," and "Fayruz Shah." He took an extraordinary pleasure in these tales, saying: "I leave the cinema to ignorant people like yourself; can the cinema offer anything to compare with a chapter from the 'Thousand and One Nights'?"

He also found in them an inexhaustible source of inspiration for the stories by means of which he sold his goods, as I was to discover later.

We—Kamal and I—knew a few words of French and English, and this enabled us to act as interpreters between al-Hajj Abdullah and the tourists whose wanderings around "The Medina" brought them to his shop.

Al-Hajj Abdullah believed implicitly in the inventions of his imagination, and in the stories which were produced by the amalgam of his abstruse reading and his sincere desire to sell his goods. One might see him buy an old wooden clog for half a lirah, which a week or two later would become the clog with which Shajarat al-Durr† killed her hus-

---

*"Al-Hajj" (The pilgrim) is a title given to those Muslims who have made the pilgrimage to Mecca. (tr)

† Shajarat al-Durr ("Tree of pearls") was the only Muslim woman ever to rule a country in North Africa or Western Asia. She assumed supreme power in the Mamluk Empire of Egypt and Syria in A.D. 1249 after the death of the sultan

52

band; or one might see him sell some poor man a fifty-year-old sword which, lo and behold, had become "al-Shakiriyyah," the famous sword of the sultan al-Zahir Baybars,* who had defeated the Mongols with it.

Similarly al-Hajj Abdullah had become the proud owner of the shirt which had been used as a shroud for Sayf al-Dawlah,† and the pipe which was smoked by the sultan Sulayman the Magnificent—and even the threadbare rug on which he had sat. "No sir, that is not for sale. That is the rug on which Saladin sat on the day he took Jerusalem from the infidels. However, for you—because you are a friend, and can appreciate the value of antiques—its price is 200 lirah; and this *nargileh* is the very one he smoked! It is a very rare antique; indeed, unique. The Sultan Salim brought it from Baghdad after he had conquered that city, and it came to me from the dome of the castle of Dolma Pasha by a way I am not at liberty to reveal . . . extremely valuable."

Among al-Hajj Abdullah's customers was a war profiteer who desired to secure acceptance in society, and he used to buy his "antiques" from time to time to decorate his home. One day this man was on the point of leaving the shop without buying anything, in spite of the fact that al-Hajj Abdullah had on this occasion excelled in inventing stories about every piece of junk in his shop.

The word "impossible," however, had no meaning for him, and so, seizing the wealthy one by the sleeve, he said: "You are a friend—a very dear friend. For that reason—for that reason only—I will show you a truly unique piece which has been dear to me, and which I had no intention of parting with. Had you not been a connoisseur of such things . . ."

He opened a drawer in a ramshackle table and took out a dull-colored silver ring with a black stone set in it. He held it up with great care between his thumb and ring finger to the pale light which filtered through the door.

"Look at this ring! See how fine it is! There is not another one like it in the world . . . unique!"

al-Sahih, her husband. When a new sultan, Aybak, was elected, she married him, and remained the power behind the throne. By 1257 she feared her power was waning, and had Aybak murdered. Immediately afterward she was battered to death with wooden clogs by the slave women of Aybak's first wife. It appears that al-Hajj Abdullah's imagination had confused the facts of history as well as the truth about his merchandise. (tr)

*The fourth Mamluk sultan (reigned 1260-1277), who inflicted a crushing defeat on the Mongols in A.D. 1260. (tr)

† The celebrated ruler of Aleppo and North Syria from 944 to 967. (tr)

The customer took the ring and gazed at it, and at the strange writing engraved on its stone. He turned it over in his hand, and finally said: "This ring is worthless—its stone is cheap and not worth a thing."

His words affected al-Hajj Abdullah as though he had been stabbed in the chest. "You must be playing a little joke, my dear sir. I don't think the value of this ring can really have escaped your notice. It has an unusual charm engraved on it."

The customer smiled ironically: "Perhaps it is the Ring of Solomon, my dear Hajj. Behold, your slave is at your service!"*

Al-Hajj Abdullah looked at him pityingly: "Rings which will bring you happiness are commonplace . . . but this one is different. It brings misfortune."

We—his son and I—were listening to the conversation. His son nudged me and whispered in my ear: "Just listen to Father when the Devil of Invention is riding him. If only he were to write fiction he would make more money from it than he gets from this business of his."

Al-Hajj Abdullah continued: "The name of this ring is 'The Destroyer of Families' . . . and this writing on it is an inscription in—er—cuneiform, meaning 'Bear children for death and build for destruction.' If you are in good health, this ring will bring you sickness . . . if you are alive it will bring you death. This ring was made by a great practitioner of magic in Babylon . . . for a prince who lived in ancient times; and he put this charm on it. It is absolutely unique. For a mere fifty lirahs. What do you say?"

"You want me to pay fifty lirahs for a ring that will bring misfortune? I can't see that it has brought you misfortune, Hajj."

The Hajj's face was a picture of pained regret. He sighed like a long-suffering man repressing exasperation: "One moment, one moment my dear sir. Give me your attention and you will learn something of advantage. I have not yet told you how this ring brings misfortune: it does not harm the purchaser at all, but if you give the ring to anyone they become liable to the most dreadful misfortunes. That is the unique property of this ring: you see, this prince fell in love with a princess who loved another prince . . . so he paid a sorcerer a huge sum to make this ring for him, and he gave it to his rival. Only three days later the rival went out hunting and was set upon by a lion, which devoured him. The princess grieved for him and died of sorrow within three days. The prince recovered possession of his ring, but one of the guards at his residence stole it."

The customer asked: "And what happened to the guard?"

---

*Solomon's Ring was supposed to confer power over all living creatures. (tr)

54

"Stealing the ring is like receiving it as a gift—it brings misfortune. A man must buy it and pay the price for it if he does not wish its evil power to strike him. The guard went on a journey and fell into the hands of bandits, who killed him and stole the ring. They sold it to a merchant in Damascus. But they had not paid for it. They were arrested and had their heads cut off. The merchant sold the ring to a young knight, but nothing happened to him because he had paid the bandits for it.

"The knight was poor, and by way of currying favor with a rich, wicked uncle he presented him with the ring. On the very same day the uncle fell from the roof and broke his neck, and the knight inherited all his wealth.

"In this way the ring passed from hand to hand. I could go on telling you its history the whole day . . . take the ring for twenty-five lirahs . . . what do you say?"

The customer replied: "I don't have a rich uncle and I don't have any enemies I wish to get rid of. And anyway I haven't got twenty-five lirahs on me."

Al-Hajj Abdullah responded to this with: "Perhaps you think I made all this up."

The customer quickly replied: "Heaven forbid!"

"No . . . no . . . I can see you think I am lying to you. You have as good as accused me openly—and I considered you a friend! I only wished to serve you and be of use to you by selling you this valuable ring for twenty-five lirahs, and you call me a swindler. That's a fine way to treat anyone!"

"But my dear Abu Kamal,* do calm down. Of course I believe you."

Finally, to pacify him, he was forced to buy a plate from which Tamerlane had eaten a meal on the day he captured Aleppo, for ten lirahs.

Later I heard that al-Hajj Abdullah had sold "The Destroyer of Families" to a certain merchant, and had made him swear not to give the ring to anyone, but only to sell it.

Then one day I opened one of the morning papers and my eye was caught by a big headline:

A RING BRINGS DEATH. The city was shocked yesterday to hear of the death of the well-known businessman Mr. ——, who was run over by a car as he was leaving his office. Rumor has it that he was the victim of a ring which brings

*Al-Hajj Abdullah's formal "honorific" name. (tr)

misfortune to its owner. He was given it by a fellow businessman, Mr. ——.

However, those who were aware of the strong bond of friendship
between the two businessmen mentioned in the paper could only treat
these rumors with the contempt they deserved. The nephew of the businessman inherited his money and the ring. He was an idle young man
and soon squandered his inheritance. He pawned the ring and forged a
number of checks, for which he was put in prison, where he died of
pleurisy.

The pawnbroker proceeded to exploit the story of the young man,
which he inflated in order to raise the price of the ring. One day he was
visited by a rich building contractor from a neighboring country, who
bought the ring for a high price and added it to his private collection of
precious stones and statuettes. But a thief broke in and stole the collection. He was seen by a policeman, and there was an exchange of shots.
The thief hit the policeman in the shoulder, but the latter shot the thief
in the stomach. He was taken to a hospital where he died horribly. The
ring was returned to its owner.

One evening this contractor's only son held a party, to which he
invited his friends. Growing merry, they dared the young man to take
the ring from his father's collection, which he did. The next morning he
got into his car to go for a run. His car was the latest model, and very
fast. At a bend in the road he lost control of the steering wheel; the car
swerved off the road and he was killed.

Overcome by grief for his son, the contractor sold the ring to the
first buyer. The fame of the ring had spread, and its price had gone up.
Connoisseurs fell over themselves to offer exorbitant sums for it—even
though al-Hajj Abdullah had originally offered it for sale for twenty-five
lirahs and found no buyer.

Time passed and my affairs kept me in Beirut. One day I was standing in al-Burj Square summoning up the courage to cross the vast sea of
blaring, racing traffic, when all of a sudden someone tugged at my
sleeve. I turned around, but for a moment I did not recognize the person who greeted me with: "Good day!" Noticing me looking hard at
him, he went on: "You've forgotten me, old chap. I'm Kamal. The son
of al-Hajj Abdullah!"

I replied apologetically, "So sorry, I never expected to see you
here—and you've changed a lot."

The fact was that he bore all the marks of wealth and comfortable
position. I asked after his father. "He has passed to God's mercy; but I
think he died happy. Do you remember the ring that brought misfor-

tune—'The Destroyer of Families'?"

My memory took me back through the years and I saw in my mind's eye al-Hajj Abdullah in his dimly-lit shop inventing fables and fantastic stories, unable to rest until he had sold something—anything—to whatever person had entered his shop.

Kamal continued: "Do you remember the legend which went with the ring?"

"Yes, I remember it very well, seeing that your father invented it in my own hearing."

He laughed. "May God pardon him. How smart he was! If only I had half his genius for invention. The legend he created made 'The Destroyer of Families' unique. People will pay me thousands of lirahs for it."

"Did you get it back?"

"Yes, I bought it through one of our agents for three thousand lirahs—I am certain it can be sold again for five thousand, and I thought Father would be pleased to see it again, when he was ill and confined to his bed. I thought I would surprise him with it one day. I told him I had got the ring, and he was mightily pleased. I said: 'Here you are, Father. You invented a legend for this ring and made a peerless gem out of a twopenny-ha'penny stone. It is worth thousands of lirahs. Here it is, as a present to you.' He thanked me for the gift and put the ring on his thumb. Then he asked me how much I paid for it. When I told him three thousand lirahs he sat bolt upright in his bed as though he had been bitten by a snake, and cried 'Oh!'

"Then he fell back dead, of a heart attack. He had been unable to stand the shock. May God have mercy on him!"

I repeated: "May God have mercy on him!"

We were silent for a moment. Then he said: "Excuse me. I have an appointment with a millionaire who wants to buy the ring. I'm going to ask five thousand lirahs for it."

THE ABLUTION

Hani al-Rahib

>>

(Translator's note: The following story alludes to the important ceremony of ritual ablution which is incumbent upon all Moslems before they pray. According to the Prophet Muhammad, ablution is "the half of faith and the key of prayer," and in the Islamic religion this essential duty of washing before prayer is founded on the authority of the Qur'an itself: "O Believers! When ye prepare your-selves for prayer, wash your faces and hands up to the elbows, and wipe your heads and your feet to the ankles." (Surah 5 v. 8) The Qur'an further states (Surah 5 v. 9): "If ye cannot find water, then take fine surface sand and wipe your faces and your hands therewith. God does not wish to make any hindrance for you." The Prophet Muhammad is also recorded as having said: "The whole earth is fit for my people to worship on; and the very dust of the earth is fit for purification when water cannot be obtained." The story is set in Damascus.)

AHMAD AWOKE GASPING. As he did so he heard the powerful voice of the muezzin: "Prayer is better than sleep . . . prayer is better than sleep." It was the voice he had heard in his sleep. He had heard it pressing close to his ears until it almost pierced them. But the words he had heard were not these. They were words which hounded him like a terrifying darkness: "Ashes and brimstone on your head . . . and in your soul black soot."

He took a deep breath, his eyes roaming around the darkness of the gloomy room. Now he could perform his ablution. He was relieved that

57

the impossibility of washing himself clean was simply a muddled dream. The suffocating sensation of dirt and uncleanliness was a nightmare. Cold coursed through his veins, and he realized that the wave of profuse perspiration had spent itself and left behind nothing but lassitude. He felt the oppressive darkness weighing on his chest; then he threw the blanket aside and switched on the light.

The room lit up, and as Ahmad gazed at the objects of the material world around him his terror subsided and he began to feel secure again. This nightmare had not been simply a dream which had vanished, for it had caused him to break out into a profuse sweat, which had exhausted him. It was such that he could only be reassured by the sight of water and the bath and soap, and he determined to have a bath immediately. The nightmare persisted, with its feeling of dense and evil-smelling black hair. Why was he overcome with this intolerable feeling of uncleanliness which did not allow him to sleep? He fingered the hairs on his arm, and felt an increasing repulsion rising up within him at the clammy softness which clung to both hair and skin.

This time he would wash himself free of it. He would rub his skin with water and soap until this dreadful layer of impurity was peeled off. It would be scoured from him and would drain away with the water into the depths of the earth. His skin would once again have its original pure whiteness, that whiteness which was so remote that he could not remember when he had last seen it. He had seen it a long time ago and longed for it. His whole being yearned for it; it yearned for it but could not find it. His whole existence had become a burden because of his uncleanliness.

He jumped out of bed lightly and quickly. He did not bother to put on his slippers. He hurried barefoot to the bathroom. He put his hand on the tap. Before turning it on he looked at the silvery water-pipe and the open mouth of the tap. A childish feeling of pleasure took hold of him, and he rubbed his arm against his hip and tucked up the sleeves of his pyjama jacket.

He turned on the tap, but no water came out. He cursed irritably. His irritation increased with the disagreeable silence. He thought to himself how any period of silence had always gotten on his nerves ever since he could remember. The tap showed no signs of life. Ahmad stood looking at it until his anger manifested itself in his hand; he turned the tap until it struck hard against its socket.

No water came out. Ahmad realized that there was something amiss with the stubborn tap. He pounded on the washbasin angrily. With a blow from his hand he forced the tap round to its furthest extent.

A fleeting, meager thread of water dribbled onto the bottom of the washbasin. Ahmad thrust forward his hands with satisfaction, to gather a handful of water. But he was unable to fill his hands as the thread of water grew thinner and thinner and then failed. He watched the mouth of the tap give a few more drops and then stop altogether. The air in the pipe gave a long convulsive gulp; then everything was quiet. The pipe was silent; so were the narrow corridor and the darkened rooms. Once again Ahmad felt the stillness. His feeling of oppression returned more strongly. It was mixed with bafflement and a reinforced desire to wash. He rushed to open the outside door and went up the steps to the roof. Quickly, with resolute steps, he went up to the water tank. As soon as he had reached it he lifted off the cover and looked in.

Perplexity now filled his whole consciousness. He no longer felt any anger or irritation—nothing but confusion. A silent creeping confusion. How could the tank be empty? He stood there. In the midst of the fresh spring breeze he was enervated by a feeling of bitterness. Needles of cold stung him and he shivered. But for the wind everything was still. The distant stars were silent. The city was silent. In his ocean of perplexity he was surrounded by stillness. As he felt the cold he looked down at his feet. His legs shivered. The feeling of uncleanliness increased, but there was no water.

He recalled to himself the dirty roof of the house, and with an imperceptible movement could see a number of people down on the pavement from where he stood. Exasperation overcame him once more, for he knew that they had performed their ablution and were now making for the mosque. Where had they found their water?

He had to wash his body in order to be able to wash his soul. A feeling of panic passed over him, lest the Prayer* should be performed and he should miss it, and another day pass without ablution, leaving the recurrent, lowering nightmare to descend on him again.

His thoughts suddenly turned to the public street, and he rushed to descend the steps. The water sources at the old public fountain from which passers-by drank and washed themselves—surely they would not have run dry? He reached the pavement, and its coldness chilled his feet as the brisk air of the street struck him. He rushed as quickly as he could toward the public fountain. He flew like the wind along the pavement. Only two things broke the prevailing stillness: the wind and himself, barefoot, fearful, and dirty. The desolate dryness, like the dryness of the wind, which he saw written on the face of the fountain shortly before he reached it, did not stop him. He resumed his running as though grasping fingers were chasing after him, or he were chasing

*The Muslim communal prayer, or *salah,* performed in the mosque. (tr)

them. He passed fountain after fountain in his questing, feverish rush, like a devotee in a frantic search for the object of devotion.

Every fountain was dry. The devout, keeping close to the walls, hurried toward their mosques. They must have performed the ablution with water; and those who had not must have performed it with dust. They had obtained water and performed their ablution. They had washed their bodies, on which they were probably not conscious of the least trace of dirt. They breathed contentment. They praised God. They took satisfaction from their cleanliness. And they made for the mosques.

He was panting. The last fountain was mocking him with the dry dumbness of the desert. He was nonplussed. He pulled with clenched fists at the handle of the fountain. He leaned on it. He eyed the fountain dully. He began to feel weak at the knees. Once again stillness. He stood stock still. Perspiration began to flow from the pores of his skin and form beads on his forehead. How could he perform the ablution now? The smell of his sweat was like the smell of stale food. He felt an overpowering heaviness.

This boisterous wind: why did it not bring clouds? Why did the clouds not gather and bring rain? Why did the twinkling stars not fade? How could the unclean continue without ablution, those who are aware of their impurity, who feel their repellent perspiration when they are awake, and who suffer deadly nightmares when they are asleep?

His hand slipped from the handle and hung loosely. He was aware that something, somewhere, was wrong. But it was still possible to perform the ablution with dust. It would be acceptable to God. The domed walls in the Mu'abbad Market could in truth solve the problem. It was not yet too late, for he was almost at the confines of the Market. Before him stood the Grand Umayyad Mosque; to his left the Zahiriyyah Library. High walls and great solid stones which no wind or rain could destroy. He put out his hand to the wall, but could not reach it. He gave an ironic smile and reached out again. He laughed at his sudden shortness of stature! He was *not* short, and had not been so before. Some demon must be increasing the distance . . .

Finally he turned away from the fountain. He put out his hand but it touched nothing. He approached the walls of the Mosque, oblivious to their mute solidity. A little dust would suffice for ablution. He rolled up his sleeves. He stretched out his palms to the massive wall of the Mosque, and was startled to see it sink into the ground. The earth simply split open to accommodate the wall's bulk, and it was swallowed up. The ground appeared as though nothing had been there. Ahmad peered in front of him, and saw the interior parts of the Mosque like the intestines of some mighty maw, exposed without any covering. They were silent and lifeless like an ancient tombstone. But it did not matter, so long as they held a little of the dust of the ground, for this would suffice to perform the ablution. He hurried to enter the Mosque.

One by one the walls sank. Every time he reached a wall it fell into an abyss. The wall adorned with mosaics fell. The wall of the prayer-hall and the prayer-niche fell. The illumining chandeliers fell. Two things only remained: the worshippers absorbed in their devotions, and the roof watching over the heads below like a sky of stone. He ran toward a wall which alone stood upright among the vanished parts of the Mosque.

He ran with all his might. His mind was filled with a resolute determination to reach it before it sank from sight. He would throw himself at it. As he saw it falling he hurled himself toward it with desperate determination. He thrust his arms out toward it, and in the next moment his middle finger touched stone. Then the wall sank, and Ahmad passed over it as the ground became level and undisturbed once more, as though no wall had been there a moment ago.

He went on running, making for the front of the Zahiriyyah Library; he saw it set in front of him like a promised land. He ran so quickly that he was no longer aware of the ground. His bare feet did not run—they flew. The wind stung them, just as it had stung his whole body, and he felt their soreness more and more. Profuse sweat poured from his body and cooled his feverishness. The wind crucified his feet. The ground became even less firm as this yawning abyss opened up to swallow the walls of the Library. Wall after wall sank into the bowels of the earth, pulled away from their rows of books. The staircases, the windows, the arches—they all sank into the earth. Even the neighboring houses, shaken violently, crumbled before the earth. Everything disappeared into the ground except Ahmad and the collection of books. He raised his face and cried out: "Oh mighty Lord, wilt thou never permit me to perform the ablution?"

He felt himself suspended in space, running, and beside him ran the books, yellowing volumes which the Imams and the commentators had filled with the legacy of their learning, and which time had filled with dust. Why were they fleeing? Were they also seeking ablution? What wall and what dust were they looking for?

A brilliant idea suddenly came to him. He marveled how he could have forgotten the thick dust covering the books—there was enough of it to perform the ablution. Like a bird of prey he changed direction and pounced upon them. He was capable of reaching them quickly. He made for them like a streaking arrow. He descended on them, his hands open, ready to grasp them, defiant, predatory and resolute.

As the books sank into the earth, Ahmad's head and hands collided with the unyielding ground, and he felt a sudden massive shock transfuse his body. From his hands and his head spurted red blood, which spilled over his unclean body. He knelt down, floating above torrents of fear and agitation, and looked at his body. He stared in supplication at the blood. The blood gushed from every vein.

Without delay he tore off his clothes and cast them away. He raised his hands to his face and rubbed it in the blood, and did the same with his neck, his chest, his back, his legs, and his arms. The blood flowed over the surface of his skin, and drops of it fell upon the ground.

At the first appearance of the morning sun he saw how his body was becoming white and pure, and how his hair, obstinately clinging to his skin, was becoming free and supple, like tender, young plants.

With deep contentment Ahmad murmured to himself: "This is the finest ablution!"

THE RAIN

Yasin Rifa'iyyah

IT WAS MORNING; the sky was clear and the sun beat down. The town was empty, as though it had been deserted by its inhabitants. The breeze played skittishly with the dust on the ground, blowing it into the air.

In the northern quarter of the town he stood awkwardly before her. She whispered to him: "Do you love me?"

"I do."

"Are you certain of your feelings?"

"Yes I am."

"Do you really mean it?"

"Yes!"

"If you are really sincere then may God send us rain!"

The young man was nonplussed; he looked up at the sky with imploring eyes, filled with anxious entreaty.

In another part of the town stood an old man leaning on a stick, looking up at the sky and smiling, for a large black cloud had appeared, and was scudding in the direction of the town. The old man cried out: "Oh Lord, our land is thirsty!"

Now the black cloud overshadowed the town, and many folk left their houses and began to stare up at the sky; some even knelt down and spread their hands toward heaven, praying for rain: "Lord, help us . . . let the rain fall!"

The cloud began to gather and thicken over the town. In the shade of a tree a brown dog stopped his barking and sat back on his hind legs, wagging his tail as he stared skyward.

The cloud continued to become more dense, until the sun's disc was hidden.

Now all the townfolk came out into the streets and peered at the sky with tearful eyes. The shaykh of the mosque and the priest from the church stood side by side, entreating: "Oh Lord, send us the rain!"

Slowly the rain started to fall. Then it began to pour. The houses of the town were deserted by their inhabitants at that moment, and everyone stood at the street corners. Each began to pray to God in his own way. In a few moments they began to run about, some of them filling their outstretched palms with the water and then washing their faces with it; others raising their faces to the sky, opening their mouths and catching water with their lips.

The rain became heavier and heavier, until the noise it made drowned all the happy voices which filled the town.

In the fields the emaciated cows, and the sheep, and the donkeys, and the dogs and the rabbits were out too, standing in the rain. It began to wash their skins clean, which long had been begrimed with dust.

The old man leaned on his stick and wept. The young people of the town began to dance and shout. The shaykh from the mosque and the priest from the church were both soaked to the skin, but they continued to stand there with eyes closed, obvious satisfaction written upon their faces.

On the northern edge of the town the young man wept, leaning his head on the mud wall, as the rain mingled with the tears running down his cheeks. The girl was staring at him open-eyed. She took hold of his hand and pressed it to her breast. Then she cried: "Oh God! . . . You love me! . . . The rain! Look at the rain watering the earth and washing the dust from the trees. It's pouring down! It's pouring down!"

The thunder began to fill the sky with its reverberations. The young man continued to sob, and began to mutter to himself, "Thank you, Lord, thank you."

The girl whispered: "You really love me . . . you love me . . . God has proven to me that you really mean it."

The young man said nothing. He raised his face skyward. Then suddenly he knelt down and began to kiss the earth . . . rubbing his forehead and washing his face. Then he stood up, and without looking at the girl, hurried toward the fields.

THE POWER OF DARKNESS

George Sālim

THAT EVENING HE WAS RELUCTANT to go back early to his empty room, because he had a melancholy feeling of depression which had no apparent cause. But he sensed that the reason for it was his attitude toward his boss—or vice versa. The fact was that he had voiced aloud his bitter dislike of the department in which he worked, astonishing his colleagues and amazing even himself. He observed in the eyes of his friends an anxious desire to dissociate themselves from him, and he read utter disapproval in their faces.

He thought to himself: "How did I find the courage for it? I've never made such a stand before!"

He very quickly realized that he had been sincere in his publicly uttered criticism, and that his friends were cowards when it came to facing the truth. Disorder and muddle were becoming commonplace in his department, and the director had forbidden his officials to say anything. He saw this as nothing less than corruption, sapping the strength of the community to which he gave his loyalty.

This feeling of oppression led him to wander aimlessly through the streets, looking at shop windows. Most of the shops were closed, but their owners had left them lit up, lowering iron grills in front of the glass to allow the observer to see what was within.

He lost account of how long he had spent wandering around. Then it occurred to him to call on some friends and while away part of the evening with them, before returning to his room. After all, he thought, tomorrow was a holiday, and his civil service colleagues did not mind sitting up late when they had a day off the next day—they could go to bed when they liked and get up at their leisure the next morning.

65

However, his colleagues' homes were a long way from the brightly-lit thoroughfares where he was wandering around, and he had to cover a considerable distance to get to their houses, which were situated in narrow streets and dark lanes. He began to feel tired, and ought to have taken a bus, but nevertheless preferred to walk, as he generally avoided traveling in packed buses except in cases of extreme necessity.

He made his way toward the narrow streets. The further he penetrated them, the more intensely the night seemed to spread its darkness. Nothing illumined the way before him but a glimmer of faint light shed by one of the grubby lamps fastened high on wooden posts common to such quarters.

His friends were numerous, and he did not have any particular one in mind; he just wanted to chat. This vagueness of intention was possible as their houses were all close together—almost jostling one another—in this old quarter.

He knocked on one of the doors and stood waiting. He waited for some time, but the door did not open. He knocked on another door. When this had no result he left it and went a few steps further on, stopping at the door of a third friend. Lights glimmered from some of the windows, indicating that his friend was home. As soon as he knocked, however, he was surprised to hear a woman's voice ask from behind the closed door, "Who is it?"

He answered with some hesitation, "I am a friend of your husband's. I've just come round this evening for a chat with him." Then he added, surmising that the woman's ear was still on the other side of the door, "Is he at home?"

The woman's low voice replied, "No. He's gone to the cinema and I don't know when he'll be back."

He began to feel irritated, and felt that he was losing his patience, but he persisted, and was soon at the door of yet another friend. Here too he noticed a dim light seeping through a crack in the shutters, and he said to himself, "There should be someone at home to have a chat with." But no sooner had he rapped at the door, the sound of the iron knocker echoing and then dying away into the quiet, deserted night, than the light went out, and a silence like that of a grave prevailed.

He waited for some moments for the door to be opened, or for someone to inquire who was there. But the door did not so much as creak, and its solid wood allowed no sound of human activity to penetrate. He remained standing perplexed in the absolute silence which faced him, and wondered what was going on.

He intended for a moment to turn around and retrace his steps to confront the cold room awaiting him, but his gaze fell upon the door opposite, and he said to himself, "Let's try one last time."

He knocked on the door, his mind made up to go home if no one were in. He felt an unbearable, miserable depression. At last the door opened, of itself, quite silently. The most peculiar thing was that the door opened outward instead of inward, almost knocking him over, and in a flash he found himself face to face with a smooth wall. He could not understand how it had suddenly sprung up and blocked his entry into the house. He put out his hand to feel what was in front of him, and his hand came into contact with smooth, solid stone.

Perplexed, he wondered what to do. Apparently this was hopeless too. He said to himself, "I'll get back home quickly. I'm tired of walking, and I've wasted half the evening. I'll have to get back to my room."

He left the open door and the smooth wall, and strode along a narrow street which led to another winding street. When he had crossed it, and the streets beyond, he would reach the main road, from which he would eventually arrive at a lane which led to his own inhospitable lodgings. He walked with rapid steps, absorbed in his own thoughts.

As he strode along, a night watchman's whistle shrilled out. It was a desolate sound, but he paid it no attention—he had heard the sound of the watchman's whistle at night countless times when returning home after a long evening out. However, when he heard a second blast of the whistle, he felt forced to turn around against his will, and he saw the watchman a short way off. He was standing at the corner of the street. The street was deserted. He wondered why the watchman had blown his whistle.

The watchman advanced a few steps, riveting him to the pavement. What did the man want? Did he think he was a thief?

But the watchman came up to him and politely—indeed respectfully—informed him: "You have taken the wrong turn!"

This baffled him. Had he ever seen him before? How did he know whether he had taken a wrong turn? Which turn did he mean?

In a soft, ingratiating tone the watchman repeated: "You have taken the wrong turn!" He pointed to the side. "This way! Not along there."

Surprise, and annoyance, overcame him. With a raised voice he said: "How do you know me? How do you know where I am going?"

After a short pause the watchman shook his head politely. "Really—this is the way. Not along there. They are waiting for you. You only have to go straight along and you will be there." Having said this the watchman turned his back and went off down the dark lane.

He thought to himself, "All right, then, this way. What does it matter? This lane leads to the main road like the others. It's only slightly longer. All these lanes come out near my room."

Thus he found himself walking along the lane as directed by the night watchman. Everything was silent and the darkness was nearly complete. Then he heard the sound of some confused disturbance, which was at first so indistinct that he paid it no attention. Soon, however, the noise became louder, and as he proceeded further down the lane it became even louder and more strident. Then a strange smell assailed his nose. He sniffed several times, and was puzzled by a certain resemblance to the tang of the sea.

His mouth parted in a smile. How could it be the sea? The town was inland, without a river, let alone the sea. He was certain that his senses were misleading him. But what was the confused sound which was getting louder? Were his ears deceiving him as well? What really baffled him was the humidity which pervaded the atmosphere: it made him perspire freely, as though he were at the seaside during a hot summer night. Then, as he was about to take his last step at the end of the alley, he was accosted by two men. It was as though they had been awaiting his arrival.

The men said, "You've arrived! It's a good thing you've come. You were sent for from the place where you live, but the man who was sent with the message has not returned yet. It's a good thing you've come."

His mouth opened in astonishment, and he exclaimed with a sudden gasp, "Come where? I don't understand a word you're saying!"

They replied, "Come with us and you'll understand everything!"

"But I don't know you. I've never seen you before!"

"We don't know you either. We've never seen you before, but that's neither here nor there."

"So?"

"You will come with us to our chief. He's the one who instructed us to bring you to him when you arrived. There you will understand everything."

Before he could utter another word one of the two men took him firmly by the arm, and he found himself walking along between them. The sea loomed up in the distance. It was an immense blue sea—deep blue. On the distant horizon the lights of small ships at anchor twinkled. He did not dare to ask any questions about this sea, but he was glad that his senses had not deceived him—the roaring sound he had heard, his perspiring, and the smell which had assailed his nose were all real.

He had always been fond of the sea. His nervousness evaporated. He was glad to see a few twinkling stars in the sky. It was as though he saw them for the first time. They walked on for a long time until they finally reached the door of a building which resembled a medieval fortress. The three of them stepped into a dimly-lit hall, and then proceeded through a series of long corridors. No one said anything. It was as though they were taking part in a funeral. He looked around him, seeing nothing but ancient stone walls. At last they came to a door from under which shone a bright light. The two men knocked on the door, pausing a moment for permission to enter. As soon as they heard a voice respond to the knock, they opened the door and pushed him inside, not entering themselves.

The first thing that he saw was the smiling face of a civil servant, who said cheerfully, "Welcome!"

Almost desperately he replied, "I don't understand all this! I don't see any reason why you should welcome me. I just want to get back to my flat, to my room."

The man did not reply. Instead he took out a packet of cigarettes and offered him one. He lit it for him, saying with complete equanimity, "Your home has been moved here." He then waved in an easterly direction, "You'll find your room there, with all your clothes and things. You will also find your books, radio, records, tape recorder and everything you need. Ask for whatever food and drink you require and they will bring it at any time you like."

He did not reply to this—it was as though he were listening to someone else's instructions. Finally he inquired, "And what about my work?"

The reply was cutting: "You gave it up last night."

Wild notions raced through his brain. He was on the point of asking, "Why? What's the point of all this?" But the words froze on his tongue as at that very moment he heard a loud noise which tore his attention away from his own perplexity. The noise was a grim combination of groaning and wailing, of snarling and barking, such as he had never heard before. A tremor passed over his face. The question burst from him, despite the now frowning face of the official, "What's that?"

The civil servant laughed, shrugging his shoulders. "It's nothing. We're near the factory."

"What factory? I know this town like the back of my hand and I don't know of any factory here."

The man came up to him, trying to soothe him, and said, "No need for alarm! This factory was built recently, in this coastal area. Its job is to produce animal pelts. The animals are brought here, dead or alive (here he gestured significantly), and are skinned with a new machine, using the most modern technology. The animals are fed into the machine, which quickly absorbs the animal and separates its skin from its flesh and bones. The head is cut off and rapidly ejected into the sea. That's why every now and then you hear some noise coming from that direction—it is the sound made by the animal as its head is severed from its body. It doesn't last more than a split second."

To this he could only reply, "So I have to stay here listening to these noises night and day?"

"You will be better off here than working in your department, won't you?"

Insistently he threw back: "No. I want to go back to my work and my empty flat."

The official shook his head with a despairing sigh.

He continued, "Anyway, how are you going to force me to stay here? Who is behind you?"

"I am simply a civil servant, who carries out his instructions. My chief has given me instructions about this and I shall carry out those instructions."

With desperate anger the other returned, "In that case I demand to see your chief."

"But my chief is simply acting on the instructions of his superior."

"Then I demand to see his superior, and I refuse to be transferred to this place."

"There's no point in that. His superior simply carries out the orders of his chief."

"Then I shall go to *his* chief."

"But he simply carries out the orders of his immediate superior."

"Then I shall just have to complain to him."

"But he again only carries out the orders of his superior."

"And who is his chief?"

"The Director."

"And who issues the orders to the Director?"

"His superior of course."

The man clutched his head in his hands, but the official hastened to catch hold of him and soothe him. "Don't take it so badly. You'll like it here, and you'll be able to retire permanently from the burden of work." He felt for the bell-button.

No sooner had he pressed it than two burly soldiers entered. He made a curt gesture to them. They saluted. "Take him to his room and don't be rough with him. His nerves are on edge." The two soldiers led him through a long series of corridors to his room. By the time they reached it his feet had gone numb with fatigue. They threw him onto his bed and returned whence they had come.

OLD ENOUGH TO BE
YOUR FATHER ...

Ghadah al-Saman

THE HOTEL GARDEN IS GROWING SLEEPY amid the ruddy glow of sunset; the crimson shadows are being pulled over the deserted wood which lies slumbering before us; they flicker over the cars parked in the square below, where women's faces gleam and mingle with the sweet sounds of the musicians in an enchanted atmosphere which wafts the dancers into raptures of delight.

My mother looks pretty in her black outfit. Her gossipy friend's tongue never ceases; it almost seems as though she has two tongues. The seat on which I am sitting is attached to the painted iron railing, and is too close to Baha's car . . . he has said they will be leaving at sunset. In a few moments they will depart, and I shall never see him again, just as my father went away a few months ago. I know where my father went. I can take a bunch of the violets he loved so much from his room to his marble tomb. As for Baha . . . at sunset he will be going somewhere where it is impossible to reach him . . .

I am disturbed by a playful laugh. It annoys me. Why do they laugh? He will be leaving this evening . . . how can they dance and philander and amuse themselves? How can the jasmine branches continue to scatter their scent about them as though nothing has happened? I am lonely. The world is a heedless and mocking whirlpool. The sun is pursuing its course across untold mountains. The night is shaking off its crimson shadows. The autumn has been intoxicated by darkness and exhales its breath in cool breezes. I shiver and shrink into my seat. I love the grandeur and the mysterious death of autumn. Baha's autumn: how I loved him! His forty-five years were a veil of profound mystery which drew me to him from the first moment, ever since my mother

71

pointed out a man in the foyer of the hotel, saying: "That is one of your father's old friends, who wasted their time playing around and traveling." I heard my mother's friend whisper in a hiss: "He must have chosen this remote resort to meet up with one of his mistresses . . . I hear that his latest is a blonde. He's coming toward us . . ."

She stopped talking as he stretched out his hand in greeting. My mother shook hands with him almost sadly, as though she wished to give the impression that his presence reminded her of my late father, and that he owed her not a few words of condolence. But his words were brief. I felt that I was in the presence of a man averse to any sort of flattery. He seemed to have a knack for burying the past without a fuss, and concentrating on the present and the future. And I was the future. The whole of his first evening he sat chatting with me and talking with me as though I had known him before I was even born. He was not restless or nervous or loud like younger men; his voice was deep and mature and full of experience. His conversation stirred up every minute of my twenty years.

When I rose to go to bed I was like a dark wood whose secret recesses had begun to glow with warmth, after vainly yearning for sunshine through long ages. And on the following day, when he came through the grove of trees in the early morning, I leapt from my seat in the garden to go to meet him . . . and to listen as he spoke of the advantages of an early morning stroll in the woods. But I did not need to be convinced; the sight of him was enough for me. And the woods were companionable.

Why doesn't my mother talk to me and rescue me from my thoughts? Why is she silent? Why doesn't she say anything to me about her memories of my father and Baha, in days gone by, as she used to all last month? Why doesn't she say to me that he was twenty-five years old when I was born? She is as silent as the grave. I wonder whether she realizes that I love his forty-five years, and not only that, but his graying hair which shines within me like the most radiant of dawns. I love his drawn face and his squandered vitality, and I love the mysterious melancholy which envelops him whenever he sits alone waiting for me . . .

He never said that the days of his life were like the waters of a stream winding through arid rocks seeking a patch of earth to irrigate . . . seeking something to create and invent. He never said that his playfulness and flippancy were searing him . . . but I understood everything that evening I watched him closely, while he was sitting alone in the garden. That night was one with winter hard on its heels, and the visitors had retired to their rooms as the first threads of darkness appeared.

He was not aware that anyone was watching him; he was looking intently at a bird hovering with parental concern around a fledgling whose young wings had failed it. A wonderfully intense concern shone in his face. Something like tears clung to his eyes, and he gave a sigh of pleasure when the fledgling gathered its strength and started to flutter once more, as the parent bird hovered around it with the solicitude of a miser. He called the hotel waiter and ordered two cups of coffee. The waiter, having brought them, looked around, puzzled, as Baha began to gulp down the first cup while he pushed the other to the other side of the table in front of the empty seat opposite him. It seemed to me as though the aroma of the ownerless cup touched his very depths with an obscure warmth. I could not disappoint him. I sat down opposite him, sensing that something was troubling him. He did not want to be taken by surprise, nor looked at intently. At that moment his inner soul was bared. Never before had a woman observed the vague shores and mysterious terrain of that private realm. I looked hard at him with a stimulating sense of curiosity and pain . . . I will never forget his face. It was profoundly bathed in a quiet sadness, like a still day in autumn. His hidden suffering was exposed like the peak of a mountain wrapped in silent, misty veils. His face was moist like a meadow watered by the refreshing showers of autumn.

It seemed to me that he was weeping through his pores, weeping with all his senses and shedding his suffering with the silent strength of an oak. I said nothing. I remained silent. After some minutes he asked: "Does my silence trouble you?"

I answered: "The sweetest words are those we do not utter; when we feel that mere syllables cannot reflect our emotions."

There was another pause, before he said softly, with disarming sincerity: "I am a master of the arts of conversation and love; but I offer you my silence. Do you accept?"

I did not reply. I did not withdraw my hand from the enclosing warmth of his, as I felt them supporting mine yet seeking support, like thirsting lips . . .

When my mother rebuked me that evening I had no room for anger. And when she reminded me that he was twenty-five years old the day I was born I felt proud and happy. I kissed her impulsively, and said: "I love the autumn, Mother," but when I had climbed into bed I did not sleep. She came into my room two hours later, apparently sensing that I was still awake. She kissed me so tenderly it aroused my apprehension. I clung to my pillow and asked her to open the window to let the scent of autumn come into the room . . . she said nothing and I felt sure that she understood everything.

Why am I recalling all this? My eyes are fixed on the big door. In a few minutes he will be coming down with that blonde of his, ready to go . . . he never loved me. He was waiting for her . . . I was just a doll for him to play with. No. I was not even his doll. Why should I deceive myself? I was a mere passing incident in his existence . . . otherwise why did we fall silent, the two of us, when we were returning from the woods a few days ago? Why did he stop stock still, almost painfully rigid, when we entered the foyer, the ancient hotel clock peering down on us like a gargoyle?

The bars of its wooden cover were like blank, vengeful fangs. It kept ticking stupidly, incessantly. Its millions of ticks crept between us. Our laughter was suddenly malevolent. The furrows in his cheeks deepened. I felt that we were shrinking as the clock expanded and its ticking grew louder. The hall was getting darker. Its walls became taller and taller and disappeared into the sky. The sky was narrow and shrunken and starless. The clock roared. We shrank, as though we had become rats in moldy, festering soil. The clock was a heathen god whose black teeth were never sated.

I put out my hand, searching for his. I found it, tired and unanimated, at his side. I clutched it. Then everything returned to its place; my mother's importunate friend said "Good morning" to us in a meaningful tone. He said with sudden harshness: "I shall not be dancing with you tonight." I did not answer. He added masochistically: "You are a child and young. You don't get tired. I am getting old. Don't forget that. Don't forget what I say."

My mother looks worried tonight. She accompanies me discreetly but discovers nothing. Why doesn't her friend gossip this evening as usual? Her face shows shadows of regret overlaid with a touch of kindness which I have never observed before. What has happened to the two of them? They jump to their feet. Here is Baha approaching with one of his suitcases. At his side is the blonde who arrived at the hotel yesterday morning. Dark clouds gather within me. Dismay. Defiance. Fate. Why is he going away? The thunderbolts and frost of winter are approaching. Why is the autumn fleeing? We opened our windows and woods for him. Why does he go away? The hearths of winter are filling our souls with smoke. The smoke tinges everything. The music and the colors and the people are plunging toward his eyes. He stands before me to say goodbye. His hand clasps mine regretfully. My mother is crying. I don't think the memory of my father is the reason. My eyes cling to his face distractedly, despairingly. His girl stands to one side. The threads of her blonde hair pierce my cheeks . . . his face fills the whole world. His face covers the sky and the whole of existence with new worlds of anxiety, resignation and otherness. Twilight is in his face. His face is shrinking . . . the blonde threads reappear.

The hubbub chatters on while my mother shakes hands with him, obscurely resentful. She does not accept his sympathy with sadistic delight, as is her wont. Her annoying friend contemplates his girl with feminine spite. I could not have believed that such a creature could be jealous. They descend to the forecourt. The play of lights slips away from his face as the interior of the car hides him from view . . . I cannot see them. She is clinging to him. She takes my place beside him. The affection in his eyes showers her with contentment and happiness.

The asphalt begins to run under the tires. The darkness swallows them up greedily. The music around me changes to a wail. Shoes are jumping up . . . and turning. Their metal heels tap upon my brain . . . implanted in my head . . . the clock looms up out of the distance . . . it gets nearer. Its wooden teeth are intent upon chewing me up. My chair rejects me. I rush off. I bump into the dancers. They stand staring at me. They keep barring my way so that the devil of the ancient clock can chew me up. I feel strangled . . . I defend myself like a wild beast whose wounds are illumined by every light in the world. I struggle. I swim in a clashing human ocean . . . they make way for me.

I continue to rush to my room. To my balcony which overlooks the valley . . . there is no noise there . . . no person . . . there is nobody to sympathize with me there.

The valley shows up deep, sad, its bottom invisible, a world of autumn, obscurity and shadows, a world of pride and silence. I wish I could fall down there suddenly. I would writhe in terror and then give myself up to space. I would mingle with the storm and the earth and the air. I am an unclean particle, my orbit isolated in a sphere of desolation and terror. I have no friend. A distant wail, sad and languishing, reaches me from the depths of the valley . . . it sobs between human groans . . . it is calling me . . . I wish I could fall down there to him . . . so that my body is scattered into warm fragments, still quivering, until they melt into the autumn. A jackal is tenderly licking its wounds.

I am a temple of fear and longing and revulsion. How I wish I could throw myself down!

A hand touches my shoulder. My mother draws me to her. I bury my face in her breast, sobbing with desolate misery. She says to me with unfeigned sadness: "From the first I worried about his deceiving you . . . but I worried more that he might be sincere . . ."

I do not reply. I continue to sob. I make her breast wet with my tears. She embraces me tenderly and says: "This is not the end of the world. You are young, and there is tomorrow."

I interrupt her with defiant stubbornness, repeating: "What do I care? Who said I loved him? He was old enough to be my father . . . old enough to be my father.

"Who said I loved him?"

EAST IS EAST

Fu'ad al-Shayib

HE STOPPED CONFUSED at the crossroads, not knowing which direction to take. Before him was the street which led to the high road. Beside him was the side road where the Odéon stood. On his right was the only other through road, from which could almost be seen the restaurant which stood at the corner. On his left was the narrow lane along which he used to saunter, alone and with hands in pockets, occasionally slipping into a bookshop. It was the same melancholy lane, reminding him of his own various uncertainties.

He stood confused, not knowing which direction to turn, although when he came down the hotel steps he had known exactly why he was setting forth this midday. Contradictory plans and inclinations jostled in his mind and prevented him from making a decision.

At one and the same moment he was bewildered and happy, lost among a thousand voices since the noontide sun had touched his face. And every voice was calling him to pleasure, to enjoyment, to life. He thought of making for the Odéon to consult the display boards for the evening's production. The books in the window of the nearby bookshop kept calling to him, beckoning and signalling. Yet he could not help looking in the direction of the restaurant, even though he had been feeling hungry for so long that he had forgotten it. But what was it he really hungered for? He looked at the ground, trying to discern what it was he really wanted.

Maybe he was longing for the company of a girl with blonde hair, on this languid, sunny, autumnal day, the kind of day which Paris rarely afforded; he would take her arm and they would go to the Luxembourg Gardens, and they would while the hours away tossing breadcrumbs to

77

the tame house sparrows which descended in flocks to the chairs of people seeking recreation there . . . he smiled at this delicious, relaxing vision, as he turned toward the bookshop window from where he imagined a voice calling to him: "Come . . . come . . . did you not promise me yesterday that you would take me away today? Did you not promise to pay for me and release me from this cold shop window, so that I could live in your pocket or the shelf above your mantlepiece?" The young man smiled again, as though he were making excuses; then he made as if to walk away, hesitated, and remained where he was.

Suddenly a taxi came by and slowed down at the crossroads. The driver thrust his head and his hand out of the window and called out rudely to the youth: "Hey, you oriental cow—can't you do anything but daydream?"

He jumped in alarm, as the car drove on and he heard the driver guffaw. Very quickly, however, he laughed, and said to himself: "It's true . . . I am like a cow! I suppose he recognized what sort of person I am from my appearance and dress, and my choosing this spot to stand in—just as though I were a cow lying in a lush pasture, ruminating and dreamily staring into space." Then he made his way toward the restaurant.

His friends used to wait for him every day there. It embarrassed him to go into public places on his own. The new life here dazzled him and at the same time confused him. He felt of consequence among his fellow students when he looked at them *en masse* at the University, or the cafeteria, or the restaurant, forming an "Arab" circle, speaking Arabic, with Arab gestures. In a moment he had joined them.

There were three of them; each one had invited his girlfriend to lunch, and they introduced them to Ahmad, who felt uncertain of himself in the boisterous circle of friends. No sooner had the girls perceived the hesitancy of the youth than they proceeded to try to draw him out, plying him with question after question.

The new arrival by no means lacked good looks, and was not dull-witted, but he felt he had a plainer face than the rest, and a simpler mind. One of his companions announced, repressing a laugh: "Ladies! Our friend here is descended from a noble Arab family, and he's a rising man of talent."

One of the girls quickly interjected: "There's no need to introduce him like that; everyone can see talent written on his face!" Everyone laughed at once.

Just then a pretty girl carrying books under her arm approached the table and greeted everyone without formality. The friends welcomed her as she went around shaking hands. One of them asked: "Aren't you going to have something to eat?"

"No."

"All right then. Won't you have something to drink?"

"No thanks."

"But . . ."

Someone else interrupted: "Do sit down anyway, so that we can introduce you to someone you'll like, our new friend here."

As the girl looked intently at him they said: "This is Ahmad." She smiled and he rose to shake hands. She took a seat at the table next to him, obviously pleased to make a new acquaintance. The rest of the gathering resumed their noisy banter.

Lucie was the third girl he had gotten to know since coming to Paris. The first had not been entirely blonde; the second had been blonde but was a chatterbox, giggling at the slightest provocation. Although he was unable to define exactly the image of beauty for which he yearned, he felt it deep inside himself. He had come across many girls in the Latin Quarter who had pulled at his heart-strings, and who had approached the image he desired, when he was going out with them, or dancing—or just staring at them. But the impressions only remained with him for a few moments, like a shadow which is cast for just a short while in a certain direction each day, or like a taxi, appearing briefly in the life of any traveler.

Lucie was the third girl whom he had come to know well enough to talk to and to share her company. He wondered to himself how it was he could talk to her so freely, and he was astonished that she should listen to him. His confidence returned.

He had fallen in love with Lucie, or rather he felt ready to love her. She reflected his vision: she was blonde, urbane, and did not mock his loneliness, nor did she break in on his pensive moods. She had a large mouth, but her smile was captivating. Her teeth were pure white: when she laughed it was as though every tooth sparkled with joy and friendliness. So why should he go out of his way to pick and choose and be critical? He had spent plenty of time in absolute deprivation, vainly seeking feminine company. He had been able to do without it for a year or even two years in Damascus, but in Paris it was impossible.

The whole world seemed to have agreed to live à deux. What a strange city! People embraced each other everywhere, in the open, under the nose of the policeman, in the hotel, in the lecture room, in church, whatever the situation and wherever the place, without self-consciousness or embarrassment, standing or sitting, in the morning, the evening and midday, before meals, after meals, before going to sleep or before breakfast. Women were everywhere. The owner of the hotel was a woman, as well as the manager and the servants. There was a woman in the store where he bought his handkerchiefs, the shop where he got his tobacco, in the café, the restaurant, the school, in cars, trams, in the métro selling newspapers, sweeping the streets, pulling carts in the fruit-and-vegetable market; so if Ahmad was overly sensitive and curious, the reason was to be found in the fact that his eyes were not accustomed to this diffusion and ubiquity of the feminine form.

Sometimes it seemed to him that women, being so universally available, were public property, like air and water. However he soon realized a hard fact: that the woman makes her choice before the man, especially if he is reserved in the various methods of introduction. Then again, how keen had been his chagrin an evening or two before, when he had heard a woman coming up to him saying: "Come on, darling . . . wouldn't you like to hold me in your arms, sweetheart?" Then it dawned on him that she was a prostitute, a seller of love, and he remembered that someone else was dear to him, yet from whom he was separated by a gulf of respect; he felt repulsion rising in him, and he fled.

He felt tormented and pained, and suffered the bitterness of loneliness, and the desolate feeling of alienation. Perhaps he should give it all up and return home on the next ship: how could he live in a paradise where all the trees were forbidden, and the only fruits offered him were fallen?

Here was Lucie who had come into his life, and looked over the horizon of his gloomy despair. She shone in his world like the Paris sunshine after an overcast sky, and here he was, tenderly putting his arm around her in the Luxembourg Gardens, living one of his cherished dreams.

She was indeed blonde, like the setting sun, as delicate as the branches of the willow, gay and laughing like the surface of a lake, as friendly and amusing as the most closely cherished book! At her side he felt as though he could burst into song—she was the song which the voice striving from his whole being sought to express. As soon as he had said goodbye to her, in the evening or at midday, having agreed on their next meeting, he would rush to the room of one of his compatriots and give him all the details of his relationship with Lucie, ending with a plea for advice.

His friend would answer: "Don't be a coward, Ahmad. Try to get her to come to your room. Usually it means a woman has yielded when she is willing to be alone in a room with her man."

Ahmad would say to himself: "What's the hurry? What's the point of it?" How could he invite her to his room like a spider inviting a fly?

Why should he pounce upon beauty as though his purpose was to seize and devour? Why should he not savor happiness gradually, little by little? When a man tasted beauty was it right for him to gulp it down without savoring the sweetness of its taste? Why should he gobble it up like a snake, when he could peck at it delicately, like a bird?

It was true that Lucie was attracted to Ahmad. But she did not utter any words of love. She listened to him talking about law and literature as though she were listening to an industrious pupil whose intelligence was beginning to flower. Partly, she was fascinated by his obvious shyness and diffidence—it was as though his eyes never looked at one without immediately looking away. These were things which were calculated to exert their charm over a woman in a fresh, reserved young man, with a sparkling mind, who was yet full of ardor.

This quiet dreamer longed to hold her as a weary man longs to find some corner where he can thrown himself down to rest. Thus she was to him a drop of moisture in a barren land, as he was to her, and a guide in a wilderness of futility. For that reason also the short period of their acquaintance seemed to be the starting point for many happy days ahead. Why was it then that his friends, whenever they saw him, would say: "What have you been up to, Ahmad? Has Lucie come to your room?"

This upset and repelled him, and he tried to avoid his friends and their idle talk. For up to now he had seen in Lucie nothing but two pure blue eyes created just like the image he had imagined, the ideal of his flights of fancy. It was enough for him to warm himself quietly in the glow of Lucie's intelligence and beauty and bask in her overflowing generosity of soul; he would devote himself to her with all the tenderness at his command, if she would confidently devote herself to him.

One evening Ahmad said to Lucie, in the tone of one who has discovered buried treasure: "Lucie—let's go to the Odéon this evening!"

Noticing the childlike pleasure in his eyes as she spoke, she replied: "What's on at the Odéon, Armad?"*

With a triumphant voice, he said: "The play *Tristan and Isolde,* the noblest and finest love story there has ever been—far superior to *Romeo and Juliet,* and more eloquent."

"That may be so," she said without enthusiasm, "but I don't really like watching the glorification of that tragic infatuation." For the first time she was speaking frankly, with unadorned opinions: "I get agitated when I watch plays of that kind; it's like eating sweet baklava, or drink-

---

*Lucie was unable, like most untutored Europeans, to pronounce the laryngeal Arabic "ḥ." (tr)

ing thick, sticky Turkish coffee. Sorry, Armad . . . have you heard of *Crime and Punishment?*"

Ahmad replied, giving in, "Of course. I enjoyed reading Dostoevsky. He was an outstanding portrayer of the restlessness of an unhappy generation, and the anxieties of abnormal minds."

"Then we'll go and see *Crime and Punishment* this evening, at the Montparnasse Theatre."

As they were watching Dostoevsky's story, she tightly holding his hand, Lucie said: "Armad . . . the actor playing Raskolnikov is almost in a frenzy!"

"How do you mean?"

"Playing this role continuously for a whole year, filled with violence and commotion, has played havoc with his nerves and shattered them. Can't you see the strain on his face: he looks positively diabolic! He has become Raskolnikov himself."

After a pause she went on: "Don't you think that a man's way of life with the passing of time in the end determines his character, even if it clashes with the real man and his genuine inclinations?"

After a silence he replied: "I don't know . . . perhaps."

That night Lucie was upset, on edge, and she did not refuse Ahmad's invitation to his room. It was the first time. She walked close beside him, pressing against his arm with her fingers. Her teeth chattered with cold, and she clung to him as though she wished to inhale the scent and warmth of the man from his body. Before they reached the hotel she spoke: "How about getting some of that strong drink you call 'arrack' in your language? I love the bitter taste of your drink. It's a good cure for headaches and colds."

"Are you showing the mentality of Raskolnikov?"

She gave a little laugh, and fell silent.

When she lay down on the wide bed in his room Ahmad thought she must be giving herself to him and calling him on. But when he came over to her he saw both her eyelids were closed and she was motionless, as though asleep. He lingered without moving, contemplating the calm face, which indicated trust in the very atmosphere of the room and the extent of his power within it. A quiver of joy passed through him as he saw Lucie before him within reach of his lips. She was his. And in the features of her calm, upturned face was the title of his ownership, signed with a soft smile.

Should he take her hot in his arms? But she was asleep . . . should he snatch her up in his hands? But he might easily hurt her . . . should he try to take her by storm with the strength of a demon?

But how innocent was this tender rose, dreaming so trustfully! How could he disturb her? Perhaps neither the thought nor the desire had occurred to her. Was one to be allowed to pounce upon her like a wild beast, and take hold of her like a ghoul, when she was under his protection and had trusted herself to his bed? No! He took a coat from the hook and covered her form carefully with it. But Lucie awoke from her daze, or sleep, and looked at the man with drowsy eyes, so solicitous of her repose. Then, without further ado, she jumped to the floor, saying: "Sorry, Armad. I didn't notice how the time was passing. I must be going," and without waiting for an answer she snatched up her hat, opened the door and rushed out with the words: "I shall miss the métro. Bye."

Her friend was left rooted to the spot, not comprehending anything of what had happened. He had wanted to accompany her on the métro as far as her house, but he only thought of this a quarter of an hour later. He felt depressed and went to bed.

The next evening she came unexpectedly to his room while he was putting some lecture-notes in order. In his surprise he asked her the reason for her rushing off the night before, and tried to excuse himself for having neglected to take her home, but she was perfectly happy and cheerful as though nothing could upset her. It was difficult to manage questions and excuses, and she had dinner with him.

It was a new turn in the life of the lovers. Now Lucie visited him every day without previous arrangement. After that evening she looked in to see him without any ceremony. Now he talked freely with her, telling stories set within a frame of the desert and camel caravans, of the moon, and flowers, and perfume and the fresh breeze—even though in reality he knew nothing of the desert life.

But Lucie's person he would not venture to touch; he hesitated even to think about it. Four evenings later he began by saying to her: "Why don't you like baklava, Lucie? Is it true that it unsettles your mind and upsets your stomach? That would be hard to believe!"

The girl laughed, and Ahmad imagined that her laugh was a sure sign his question had made an impression. But he did not hear the slight grating of her teeth, or notice the tensing of her jaw muscles. She fell silent and leaned on the table, resting her chin in her hands.

He said: "Do you feel all right?"

She replied: "I don't feel well."

Feeling ill at ease he said quickly: "Shall I get you an aspirin?" She thanked him and then got up to go. He accompanied her to the métro.

Five nights later Ahmad gave her his photograph as a present, signing it with a few well-chosen words, which Lucie repeated to herself with pleasure—they were couched in poetry, for which she had a compulsive love. He showed her a collection of his photos, with photos of Damascus, and photos of his father and mother and brothers and family. He always felt the need to produce something new when the two of them met, however trivial it might be. He was disconcerted when this became difficult and he noticed her nervously twisting her lower lip.

Six nights later talk about the East led to the subject of the advantages of circumcision, and the desirability of this operation for the sake of hygiene. Lucie asked: "And you, Armad . . . are you circumcised?"

He laughed loudly as though the question tickled him: "Of course." Then he looked away in embarrassment.

She sat staring at him.

The seventh evening was such as he had never enjoyed in his life before. He had danced with Lucie until dawn. For the first time he gave her a long kiss. He put his arm around her and walked home with her in the early hours of the beautiful blue Parisian morning. He felt he had immersed himself in her company enough to last a long, long time but when the sun was fully up he found he already missed her.

Ten days later Ahmad brought home a fine bottle of Bordeaux, which he placed on the table, and then sat down to wait. When she arrived she shouted with exaggerated astonishment: "Oh! Who are we drinking to this evening?"

He gave a ready answer: "To our love."

The girl demurred in a pleasantly mocking tone: "That's too much . . . and too formal! Don't you see what I mean?" He looked down uncertainly as she went on: "Don't you think it would be better to drink to the East, the caravans, the night, the moon?" Then she raised her red glass in her slender fingers for a moment, as the first glimmerings of dawn began to flicker. She swallowed it in one draught. Then she started to laugh, as though the wine had no sooner touched her stomach than it had risen to her head. Her mood in the course of the evening was one of amusement, overbearing mockery and petulance.

The more her temper rose and the sharper her tone, the more yielding and quiet Ahmad became. The blood rose to her cheeks, making them flare, and made her ears pink, like two rose petals set among the sparkle of her fair hair. Her mouth looked as though it had been freshly painted, craving for more wine. Her eyes were covered with a filmy moisture, and their blueness was more intense, as though suffused with elation. She laughed at everything Ahmad said, and took pleasure in repeating: "I don't believe a word of it!" If he assured her that it was so, and swore to the truth of it, she would burst out laughing.

She tapped with her feet on the floor and with her hands on the table, as though she were dancing while sitting, or trying to fly with her limbs in fetters. There was nothing that could please him more than to see her smiling radiantly, overflowing with gaiety and whimsical high spirits.

Suddenly she gave him a sharp tap on his shoulder and called out: "Armad . . . will you dance?"

He replied, taken aback: "Yes, with pleasure, but how can we dance without music?"

"What do you want music for? I'll whistle for you and we'll dance in time with it!"

But she had not danced more than a few steps when she released herself from his arms and flung herself onto the sofa. Her face had begun to change color, from a dull dusky red to a pallid white of an indefinable strangeness. As she sank back listlessly on the sofa her dress was drawn back from her knees, revealing part of her thigh, pink as though burned by the sun, or suffused with wine.

The young man saw this from the corner of his eye, and although she noticed this she did not move her hand, paying no heed to this display of her attractive form. She allowed her hands to hang limply at her sides, as though she were floating in space, unconscious. Her dress gradually moved up her legs, slowly and noiselessly, until her body, so elegantly displayed, seemed to cry out.

It occurred to him that perhaps he should draw her attention to the way she was sitting, but he refrained out of regard for her feelings and to avoid embarrassing her. He half turned away and averted his eyes, as though making a silent response of honor to Lucie's trust in him. For if she had not trusted him completely she would not have allowed herself such free and easy behavior.

However, in another minute Lucie's arms were around his shoulders, and her head fell on his breast. He was startled and nonplussed and cried out: "Lucie! Lucie! What's come over you?"

Breathing heavily, she replied: "Nothing . . . nothing."

In confusion he asked: "Has the wine gone to your head?"

Like a child in the midst of a dream she answered: "I don't feel well."

Then she lifted her head away, and flung herself onto his bed as though in a fever of exhaustion, as though she had been engaged in a combat which had drained away her blood and fatigued every fiber of her body. She lay on the bed, instinctively soft and compliant, like a ripe fruit which has fallen from a tree onto the grass, in the shade of overhanging branches.

But he—Ahmad—could not comprehend what was happening. Everything he saw aroused in his heart a flood of intoxicated love. In this giddy state of emotion he could not stop to think, or ask anything more. He overflowed with a happiness like the sea poured into a cup, but he was overwhelmed and perturbed.

Eleven evenings later Ahmad waited for Lucie to appear at his lodgings as usual. But she did not come. He did not see her on the twelfth evening. He wondered to himself, but was not worried. Then he began to feel uneasy, and apprehension took hold of his heart when after waiting two more days Lucie still had not come.

Five days later he set off early in the morning to the students' quarter, scrutinizing the faces of those who might know Lucie, or whom she might know. Her friends denied any knowledge of her whereabouts—his friends laughed at him when they saw him miserably wandering from café to café, visiting one restaurant after another.

He was so beset by longing and anxiety he was almost beside himself. He began to think he was ill. Perhaps he was contracting consumption—he was inhaling factory smoke all day, as he lived almost on top of a belching factory chimney, in a country which was covered with fog, and where the sun only came out once a month, if one were lucky. He had no appetite for European food, which had no fat or salt in it, and he was repelled by the spectacle of the millstone of the great city grinding millions of human bodies. So what was the point of studying? Did he have to come to study in this atmosphere of din, dust, and fog? It seemed to him that he had come for nothing, except to see Lucie. He would go home if she would go back with him.

Then by chance he came across a sheet of paper on which one day she had written her address, before love had bound them together. Up to now he had paid no attention to her address; now he determined to write to her:

> Lucie! Where are you? Can you understand how desperate I am? Where are you? Are you ill? Have you gone away and forgotten me? Have you left me as a joke, or seriously? I don't understand you. You gave every indication of returning my feelings; so how can I reproach you? And for what? Where are you living? What are you doing? I am living in the noisy, smoky hell of your city, and have sworn I will stay here as long as you are by my side! Your city is crushing me! Its millstone is grinding my bones. I feel as though I am choking and going mad in loneliness. I am waiting and waiting every evening and every morning, every hour, every minute, for you to come back.

He had to contain his impatience for three days before he received a reply:

Kind Sir,

I have been visiting an aunt in the suburbs, and read your kind letter today when I returned, and am replying without delay.

All I ask of you is that you will refrain from thinking about me, looking for me, trying to get in touch with me and writing to me.

I have a reason, which you may or may not be aware of . . . it's all the same to me. I do not say: "I love you"; it is stronger than that: I hate you. If I were to see you again I should feel sick and nauseous, as though I were spitting out baklava or Arab coffee. I think if I were to go out with you again I should feel like someone lost in the desert with only the sound of camel bells for company. As for the millstones grinding your bones, I would be only to glad to dance on them. Poor fellow, my lungs are used to breathing in smoke, so much so that I should miss it. How I pity you! I say to you now—don't wait; don't hope, and don't think about me, because I shall not come back to you.

Allow me to return your beautiful photograph, which you gave me one evening with the eloquent dedication: "To you my angel . . . I present the picture of a man . . ."

Unfortunately, my good Sir, I am not an angel . . . and you are not a man. Goodbye.

AN ACCIDENT AT "THE PALACE OF HAPPINESS"

Fadil al-Siba'i

THE LANDLORD OF "THE PALACE OF HAPPINESS" was having an argument with a gentleman who had just arrived seeking a bed for the night, when he heard the tapping of a stick on the stairs, followed by a voice calling out to him:

"Landlord! Dahi al-Hamdan!"

He recognized it as the voice of Shaykh Jasim ibn Ali al-Ta'ban, who had come in to the county town from his village to do some shopping. The Shaykh entered, panting from the discomfort of traveling and the effort of climbing the stairs. He had a short gray beard and wore a thin black headband over a dusty white *kufiyyah*. He had removed from his emaciated frame a thin, faded, woolen cloak which was ragged at the hem.

Dahi al-Hamdan, wishing to finish his argument with the gentleman, who so far had not given his approval to any room at the inn, welcomed the new guest:

"Do come in, Shaykh Jasim, and welcome!"

The Shaykh came inside, tapping the floor with his stick and murmuring a blessing on the house, repeating: "Give us strength, O Lord, give us strength!"

Dahi welcomed him cordially, for he had a feeling of respect for his age. Then he led him up to the roof—yes, the roof: this was not the first time he had made up beds for guests on the roof when the inn was full. Access was gained to it by means of a small door at the end of the hall. He did this every summer, and indeed whenever the number of guests exceeded the number of beds in the rooms. The sky was clear and full of twinkling stars: so why should he begrudge his guests sleeping under it, where they could enjoy the mild air? After all, people sleep on the roof when they are at home; why should they not do so when staying at "The Palace of Happiness"?

True, Dahi al-Hamdan was careful to bear in mind the warning of Sergeant Abd al-Hasib, the obstinate local policeman with the ragged sandy moustache, who, whenever he passed by the inn on summer nights and saw guests in their beds on the roof after nightfall, would shout out to Dahi, threatening to take him to the police station if he committed this offence again.

The Sergeant's warning was prompted by the very unlikely possibility that one of the guests sleeping on the roof might wake from his slumbers in the small hours and, because of the darkness and his own sleepiness, might miss the way to the small door leading to the hall and bear to the left—in the direction of the market place—and fall headlong to the ground, never to wake again!

Sergeant Abd al-Hasib had cautioned him and warned him and threatened him, but on each occasion had been content merely to caution. Dahi on his part listened each time with care to the policeman's point, and made a show of expressing his determination to follow his advice, admitting: "Your concern is perfectly reasonable, officer."

Or sometimes he would seize the opportunity presented by these warnings and would add in a confident tone: "Rest assured, officer— I've been running this inn for thirty-two years, and there's never been a single accident on that roof!"

Then the policeman would begin warning him again, and Dahi would reiterate that he would do as he required the next time . . .

Dahi al-Hamdan bore all this in mind. He bore it in mind as he led his guest the Shaykh up to the roof, with the moon shining like a great torch in the sky. But as on every previous occasion when he recalled the policeman's warning, he felt no qualms about what he was doing. For as long as he could remember he had been propelling guests up to the roof of "The Palace of Happiness," and not one of them had ever had an accident! So what possible cause for concern was there?

Shaykh Jasim ibn Ali al-Ta'ban took off his cloak and *kufiyyah* and extricated himself from most of his clothes. Then he lay down on his bed. A feeling of relaxation gradually crept into his limbs after his journey, which was admittedly not very long, but he had had to wait for a car to bring him from the village and had contracted a backache, which caused him considerable pain.

The roof, right next to the tops of the ancient mulberry trees in the courtyard of the neighboring *khan,** was bathed in moonlight. To his weak eyes the sky with its shining full moon appeared absolutely clear. He repeated to himself several Koranic verses in praise of God's omnipotence in raising these sublime heavens, decorated with glittering stars, and he recited aloud the Profession of Faith in God and His Prophet.

As he lay in his bed breezes blowing in from the distant sea wafted about him. In his imagination he saw his young daughter Khadrah back in the village, saying goodbye to him as he mounted his donkey and rode off toward the high road. Her face had been shining with happiness. Yes, Khadrah was very happy at this time, and so was he. She was soon to be married. He had betrothed her to Hammud, the cousin of the local squire, for a large dowry. He had gone to great pains to secure this dowry, for he was aware how precious the daughter he was giving away was to him: she was the last to leave the nest.

All his other daughters were married, and the sums paid out on marriage by an equal number of his sons had been provided for by the dowries the daughters had received. Now Khadrah alone was left, and the whole of the dowry would be his, without the burden of sharing it with a son who wished to get married.

Tomorrow he was going to buy Khadrah a blue dress and a frontlet of ten gold coins to wear on her forehead on her wedding day. He was going to buy a dress for her mother, too. He was also going to try to purchase three milch-cows, which would give him milk and be useful for ploughing.

The breezes from the direction of the sea continued to blow upon him; slumber bathed his eyelids, and they closed over his sleepy eyes with their reddened rims . . .

Thus he gave himself up to sleep as the full moon slipped down toward the west, its immemorial setting-place.

The Shaykh had no idea how long he had been dreaming of the cows he was going to buy, which would bring him wealth and plenty, when he awoke and felt the need to get up. The moon had set in the west and its silvery light had vanished. Only the stars shed their feeble light from the high heaven.

The Shaykh got out of bed and his feet felt their way to the door leading down to the hall. At first he was unable to find anything, but then he began to feel carefully along the wall in an effort to locate it. The door, however, was reluctant to reveal its position, and the Shaykh

---

*An inn, usually consisting of a large quadrangular building enclosing a courtyard, where caravans put up. (tr)

went on groping at the wall in his search for it. The door continued to hide itself, as though wishing to mislead him, but his need was pressing, and the Shaykh persisted in his search along the wall for the elusive door. Then all of a sudden he felt one of his feet treading upon thin air and his other foot followed suit . . . in a trice he was lying on the ground in the market place in the pitch dark, without a soul being aware of his presence there.

The gentleman with whom Dahi had been arguing earlier lay sleeplessly in his room, disgusted with this inn where he had been forced to put up for the night—it was devoid of any pretence at cleanliness. He had had a long argument with the landlord concerning his desire to secure a single room with a clean bed, but Dahi—as he heard the other guests address him—had insisted that this bed was the best one in the whole inn. In considerable irritation he had retorted: "Now just look, Mr. Dahi—look at this sheet! It's covered with grime. It hasn't seen hot water and soap for months!"

Dahi had replied, turning away: "If there is any other vacancy in the town you have only to go there."

As there was no other vacancy he had been obliged to spend the night at "The Palace of Happiness," cursing the perverted whimsy of the landlord which had inspired him to grace his inn with such a pleasing name. It would have been more appropriately called "The Caravanserai of Squalor"!

As he tossed and turned in his bed, he became aware of a strange noise coming from the direction of the window, which overlooked the market place. At first he paid no attention to it, but reverted to thinking about his present disagreeable situation. Then there came to his ear several low moans, which died away, only to be followed by a man's voice reciting the Confession of Faith. He wondered who it could be, whose heart had thus suddenly been overwhelmed by a surge of faith in the early hours of the morning, and was now wandering around reciting: "I bear witness that there is no deity but God," and so forth.

The voice, however, continued to reach him from the same distance of only a few yards from the window, without its owner proceeding on his way. It was varied with inarticulate groans and plaintive moaning, which reached the puzzled man as he lay sleepless on his bed. A confused idea, which he quickly dismissed, came to him: had someone been passing through the square and been struck down by an assassin's hand beneath the window, and now lay reciting the Confession of Faith before breathing his last?

The voice from the nearby square quavered: "Dahi! Where is the landlord?"

It seemed the matter was more serious than he had thought. He jumped out of bed and ran to the landlord's room. He woke him up and told him there was someone calling for him down in the square.

As he returned to his room he heard the landlord go out into the square and let out a shout of astonishment. The next moment he could be heard humbly addressing the man: "Why are you here, Shaykh Jasim? Weren't you upstairs?"

*　*　*

In the wake of the accident the guests of "The Palace of Happiness" were soon astir, for news of what had happened, and the ensuing hubbub awakened every one of them. The news also reached—Dahi never knew how—the night-watchman at the top of the street. The inn swarmed with wakened guests and policemen, all seeking to get a look at the Shaykh who had fallen from the roof into the market place in his sleep.

Shaykh Jasim ibn Ali al-Ta'ban was put back into bed in a semi-conscious state, hearing all around him the gasps of astonishment, without fully realizing that it was he who was the cause of them, and that he was already the begetter of an absorbing story which was immediately passed on by each person who heard it.

One of the policemen approached the Shaykh to feel his pulse. An inevitable question was quickly posed by an inquisitive onlooker: "Is the Shaykh dead? Is he dead?"

The policeman looked up and announced in relief: "No . . . he's not dead."

Dahi kept stealing fearful glances at the door leading to the hall, afraid that Sergeant Abd al-Hasib would choose to arrive on the scene at this very time when his prediction had come only too true. When he heard the policeman's assurance that the Shaykh was not dead, he felt his confidence return and he breathed a deep sigh of relief, for if the Shaykh had not died immediately after falling off the roof, it was unlikely that he was going to expire slowly now.

As reassurance spread among the crowd on the roof, the gentleman was still relating the story as he had witnessed it himself with obvious relish: "Then after that . . . I heard what seemed to be a body crash to the ground. At first the person began to groan. Then he said: 'I bear witness that there is no deity but God, and I bear witness that Muhammad is His Servant and His Apostle.' As he said this it seemed to me as though he were breathing his last—I said to myself: 'The man must be dying.' Then he cried out for Dahi. So I jumped up straightaway to fetch Dahi . . . I said to him: 'Go down to the square, Dahi, there's a man there calling for you!' "

As the Shaykh began to come around, someone began to feel his arms and legs. He announced that the patient was quite all right and that he had suffered no fracture or lesion, or even a scratch. During the examination and probing the Shaykh could not restrain his impatience with the operation, and kept saying in exasperation: "There's nothing wrong with me . . . leave me alone . . . I want to sleep!"

One of the policemen put forward a suggestion: "The Shaykh ought to be taken to the hospital—he may have suffered some internal injury we don't know about. It might carry him off before the night's out and we shall be responsible."

This idea did not appeal to the Shaykh, for he felt no pain and wanted to sleep. "Please leave me alone, everybody, I feel very tired. I want to get some sleep."

The policeman inquired: "Which village do you come from, sir?"

"There's nothing wrong with me . . . leave me alone!"

"I would just like to know which village you come from, sir."

Scarcely had the Shaykh given the name of his village than the night-watchman, standing behind him, shouldered his way toward him through the crowd around the bed, saying: "So that's where you come from, Shaykh? What is your name, sir?"

He looked hard at his face in the darkness. The night-watchman was from the same village. The Shaykh replied: "Jasim—son of Ali al-Ta'ban."

The night-watchman fell on him and embraced him, as he had recognized in him a friend of his father's. He insisted on taking him to the hospital to spend the night, as a precaution against possible internal injury.

* * *

Dahi al-Hamdan did not notice the weight of the body he was carrying to the nearby hospital. Shaykh Jasim was unable to stand upright, let alone walk to the hospital, and so the night-watchman had told Dahi to carry him there. The Shaykh was as light as a feather—he seemed to be nothing but skin and bone.

All the signs indicated that the patient was perfectly well, except for his inability to walk, which no doubt had been caused by the great fright and shock which he had suffered.

The Shaykh was put into bed and entrusted to the care of a nurse with blue eyes, which widened with astonishment when she was told the story of the accident. This increased her solicitude toward him, and the duty houseman was called. He was roused from his bed in a somewhat irritable frame of mind, but this disappeared as soon as he heard the unusual story, since its oddness intrigued him.

The Shaykh was not in any pain. Perhaps there was a little discomfort, but the shock he had suffered had diverted his attention from it. The night-watchman was very solicitous toward him; he persisted in plying the blue-eyed nurse and the houseman with questions, to get at the truth of the case.

After he had examined him, it became clear to the doctor that the Shaykh had suffered an internal injury; there was severe internal bleeding . . .

The Shaykh, stretched out in bed, slowly became aware of the reality of the pain throbbing inside, and felt the onset of a haze of unconsciousness. Through it there appeared to him his daughter Khadrah, saying goodbye to him at the edge of the village . . . Khadrah, the last one to leave the nest . . . to be married shortly . . . he had already received her dowry . . . he alone would enjoy the dowry . . . he would buy three cows, and many other things!

The internal bleeding became worse as he sank into unconsciousness. His soul slipped away, through the windows of the hospital, to a higher place . . . but in its flight it paused for a moment over his village, to take leave of sons and daughters and grandchildren, as they awaited the Shaykh's return from town with all the necessary paraphernalia for the coming celebration.

* * *

Dahi al-Hamdan awoke early.

He had not yet learned of what had happened to the Shaykh. He had left him at the hospital perfectly safe and sound. He had given thanks to God for the satisfactory outcome. If the Shaykh had died he would never have escaped the clutches of Sergeant Abd al-Hasib. If the Sergeant attempted to blame him for the night's accident he would reply: "But the Shaykh was not killed. You have no need for concern. I took him to the hospital and he was sound in wind and limb."

Then he added, talking to himself: "And so there is absolutely nothing for you to say in the matter, Sergeant. May God spare me your unwanted presence!"

Yes, that was the answer he would give him. But he would not go back to doing things as before. He was afraid that the next time a fall would bring about someone's death, and the Sergeant would seize upon

it as an opportunity to bring him to account and haul him into court!
No, he would not go back to doing things as before, after today . . .
never!

THE WRATH OF SHAYKH MUHAMMAD AL-AJAMI

Nabil Sulayman

i

PALLOR HAS PREYED ON THE FRESHNESS of her face. Yesterday her cheeks were flushed with the bloom of vitality. As she slipped behind me today she whispered: "I shan't be coming tonight." I turned quickly and rebuked her for being so shy, but she replied meaningfully: "You know I was not frightened last night." Then she fled.

"The hornets are buzzing around me"—that is how Sukar likes to refer to these men, both young and old, when the April day sets the blood coursing.

Faru's house cannot hold all the guests; but this carpet laid outside will do as well. There are ten vegetable patches in front of his clay-walled house. The earth is a smooth carpet blooming like a baby's cheek. April scorches even the blood of the earth . . . the tables will be set out here. Faru has ritually slaughtered three full-grown beasts—Shaykh Muhammad al-Ajami would not be satisfied with less!

When the Shaykh, who has lain beneath his domed shrine for a thousand years, is wrathful, evil pervades the skies over the little mountain village. Not only your house, Faru! Let us ward off his wrath with sacrifices and alms and intercession . . . yes . . . for no sooner is Shaykh Muhammad al-Ajami satisfied than the world smiles and doors are thrown open.

ii

The last ruddy threads of the sun's rays have vanished and the line of the horizon in the west, looking out to sea, has begun to disappear.

The night is moonless.

I am waiting beside you, Shaykh Muhammad. Sukar will come at nightfall. I shall not let her go this time . . . come what may . . . right in your shrine, Shaykh Muhammad, we shall . . .

iii

In the early morning, when Faru knocked at our door, the sun was still hiding behind the eastern mountains; I heard him confide to my father his disappointment at his visit to the holy Shaykh. We recited the opening words of the Koran while we listened for news of the door, which had not opened. Father suggested an immediate meeting of the elders.

Ali al-Barghut said: "Faru is a righteous man."

And Shaykh Latif said: "Faru always prays the ritual prayer at evening inside the shrine itself!"

My father said: "Ever since this village existed our Lord Shaykh Muhammad has been its proprietor . . . oh God avert from us Thy wrath and the Shaykh's wrath as well!"

Faru said, as the atrocious misdeed gnawed at his heart: "What is your opinion on this matter, brethren?"

The brethren resolved to make a solemn vow over three sacrifices: these hornets, Sukar, made a condition that they should attend the banquet of propitiation and the prayers for forgiveness. Perhaps Shaykh Muhammad may extend forgiveness, so that the world will laugh again and the door be open.

iv

Amused by my insistence, she said: "Do you realize what my being divorced means? I shall become pregnant if you . . . do you realize what my becoming pregnant would mean? You are not interested in marriage now . . . it doesn't matter . . . but anyway you would not get married to a divorcée . . ."

I said: "This time we shall be one, in the shrine itself . . . the night and the shrine shall protect us . . ."

And when she came I was still waiting for the sun to set, as lovers have always done. I rushed into the shrine. God bless you, Shaykh Muhammad. Shooting stars have been falling upon you all night, to light up your tomb and to honor your shrine. Many foreheads have bowed low to touch your threshold, and many lips have kissed its dust, but today you will be receiving two very different visitors.

Sukar pushed open the old low wooden door—then shrieked like a startled night bird.

In the midst of the intense darkness within, the specter of the tomb's inhabitant was rising over us, taller and taller, swaying to and fro like a serpent.

The smell of the incense filled my mind with childhood memories of the stories told about the inviolability of this place, about its sanctity, about the character of its occupant as a mediator between God and man, about the local beliefs . . . Sukar pushed me back . . . I held her tightly round the waist, but she twisted out of my clutch and darted from me.

She closed the lid of the tomb and rushed back to me, clinging to me. I saw her eyes in the gloom, and they were closed, betraying terror. I kissed her but my throat went dry. The blood had left her cheeks. I felt a creeping dread taking hold of me, which was sapping my desire and destroying my resolution. I buried my fingers in her hair and she pressed herself to me frantically. Little by little Shaykh Muhammad al-Ajami began to disappear from our gaze . . . his snake-like form became less terrifying. Sukar swayed for a moment like a flickering flame and then fell against me so that I almost fell over. As I recovered my balance I became aware of a muttering noise, and I saw her let go of me in horror. The lid was beginning to open a second time, and my hair stood on end . . . I tried to push it back, crying out in a strangled voice: "Help me . . .!"

But she had fallen at my feet on the sacred threshold, and I felt my strength draining away. I shouted out again: "Help me, Sukar!"

I heard her say faintly, with the voice of someone emerging from the grave: "He's behind you!"

I turned around, wanting to cry out: "It's coming at me from all sides!" But my tongue would not move. The lid had almost defeated my exhausted arms when Sukar pulled herself to her feet, and we united our strength against the ancient wooden frame to form an immovable barrier. After a deathly pause, which seemed to last an eternity, we heard a sound like footsteps receding, and in the surrounding gloom we were left contemplating the tomb and the recumbent Shaykh beside us and our two selves.

Then we flung ourselves over the threshold, relieved, frustrated, and terrified.

v

At the front of a solemn procession walked Shaykh Latif, my father, and all the notables of the village, Faru being among them, while behind them walked the young men and the children. At the very end came the womenfolk.

I looked for her in the ranks at the rear. The people had already eaten of Faru's votive offering, while the old people had offered a prayer for forgiveness led by Shaykh Latif. All that now remained to be done was to present themselves at the affronted shrine.

But before the solemn procession could get there I had seen her eyes laughing at a distance. I contrived to get close to her. I was glad to see her laughing as though nothing had happened.

She said: "The door will be opened this time!"

I replied, almost touching her: "Do you realize that there is another pair of secret lovers in the shrine?"

She answered: "But there are too many this time . . . it won't do any good for the two of them to resist."

My hand searched for her fingers in the pressing and anxious bustle of the crowd, and scarcely had we hugged each other than we heard shouts of "God is most great!" and "There is no deity but God!" from the front of the procession.

A voice was raised: "The wrath of the holy one has departed. Praise be to Thee, oh Lord! Your offering is acceptable, oh Faru!"

And behind us some of the women began to utter shrill cries of joy.

THE BUTTERFLY COLLECTOR

Muzaffar Sultan

THE LABOR PAINS WERE UPON HER . . . the unborn child remained obstinately in her womb, day after day, until it had almost reduced her to a living corpse. It changed the little group of women around her to anxious ghosts, flitting to and fro restlessly with pale faces and white lips, forever dwelling on the age-old pain they were enduring and would go on enduring. They prayed fervently for the baby to be delivered.

The labor pains were upon her . . . the child resisted them, and from the mother, with the eyes of a martyr, came screams and strangled groans, as her once beautiful and appealing features were contracted and distorted with the ebb and flow of the pain. Her breath came with difficulty. She prayed fervently and sighed. She fell into a troubled doze, only to awaken once more with imploring cries on her lips.

No . . . it is not an easy thing to transplant one body from another, to separate soul from soul, for one life to become independent of another.

He gave his first cry . . . she heard it as it pierced the unbearable pain, like a flashing knife in the dark. The faces of those present relaxed and beamed with joy—all except for her face, which was stamped with the submissiveness of the innocent as she lapsed into unconsciousness and went into a deep sleep.

Some hours later she awoke, with the memory of that age-old cry which would remain with her for ever after. The women took their leave one by one. At last she could be alone with the one who had given that cry and look into his eyes, one smiling morning. In them she saw her own soul, renewed, peering up at her; in them were herself and his father, smiling joyfully. And in his eyes she saw many other scenes; or perhaps, in her state of happy exhaustion, in her imagination.

She saw that first meeting, with him waiting apprehensively at the corner of a deserted street on a dull, rainy winter afternoon.

In those two eyes which as yet were innocent of meaning she saw the whole significance of her life. In them were the gentle gusts of the breezes of hot summer evenings, and in them were the little smiles which they were wont to exchange, seated opposite each other on the wide balcony of the friendly old home.

In them she could see the quick kisses of morning and the passionate kisses of evening and what lay between.

She saw in them, or in her imagination, successive precious things—the face of his father, stern and glowering in anger, calm and generous at times of relaxation and pleasure.

In them she saw the freezing December nights when they happily cuddled under thick blankets seeking delicious warmth and drowsy kisses.

At this moment his father came in and with a kiss wakened her from her dream of a kiss. He picked him up in his arms and looked into his eyes. She was rapturously happy. Would he find in those eyes what she had found a few moments ago?

She was so happy she could have cried. What poor simpletons were they who claimed that there was no aim or meaning in life!

The days passed like the counted beads of a beautiful rosary. The child began to crawl, and her heart began to crawl after him. And when he stood upright, a merry, reckless child running and tripping here, there, and everywhere, her heart ran and tripped after him.

He grew older and one prank followed another. The yard of the house was no longer big enough for his constant mischief and never-flagging play, and he would slip away into the little garden behind their house, then into the neighbors' garden, which was larger and more luxuriant, and then into all the neighboring gardens. He would penetrate their little paths and thickets, and his mother would be afraid of him tumbling or being bitten by insects.

She would reproach him with a frown which almost took refuge in a laugh. Then he would jump up to her willing neck like a cat and kiss her lovingly, as though trying to snuggle back inside her. This would efface what had happened, and kindness would cancel misdeeds.

One mid-day in early spring the boy ran to her joyfully with a beautiful little butterfly in his hand. She had been sure he would come back safely, but the length of his absence had made her anxious. She pitied the innocent little insect in his innocent little hand. He was bound to hurt it, even though his was the hand of a child. She took it from him gently, and having helped it to regain its balance, set it free. This displeased him, and he brooded over it inside his young soul, young and fresh like the wings of the butterfly.

Two days later he brought her two more butterflies. One of them did not move. She released the one that was still alive. She kept the other as an instrument with which to reproach him, which she did at some length, admonishing him and saying: "Promise me you will never catch butterflies again!"

"But Mother, I love them!"

"But darling, people do not kill things they love!"

"I did not kill it, Mother; it just died in my hand."

His mother thought for a while before she asked him: "Do you love me, Farid?"

The boy thought for a while before answering her: "When you don't scold me . . . yes."

His mother smiled, and felt prepared to hug him hard and kiss him, even if he insisted on catching every butterfly in the world. But she took a restraining hold on herself and kept to a tone of light-hearted seriousness: "I won't scold you again. And you won't catch butterflies again or torment them ever again . . . are we agreed?"

"Yes . . . but . . ."

At this point one of the neighbors called in, and the conversation was broken off; and the butterfly collector broke the agreement which he ought to have kept. All the gardens and fields and riverbanks, near and far, became his pleasure-grounds, his hunting-grounds.

Neither the displeasure of his mother nor the frowns of his father were sufficient to check him in pursuing his favorite sport. In his room you might find whole collections of butterflies, and even his mother and father and their relatives could not refrain from looking at them and admiring their beautiful appearance, and the way they were displayed.

It was a stifling evening not long before the height of summer, and the little family was sitting on a broad balcony trying to enjoy a slight breeze from the north. The mother kept urging her nodding son to go to bed. Fighting to keep his eyes open he declared he did not yet feel sleepy. His father sprang up and said firmly: "No, let him stay here. Let him listen to me."

The boy tried to pay attention through the soft veils which sleep was beginning to draw over his consciousness, as his father rapped out: "Farid, you are going to stop catching butterflies from now on!"

"Yes, father."

"You are not going to do any more butterfly collecting after today. Do you hear what I say?"

"Yes, father."

"You will get rid of these butterfly collections of yours. You have wasted far too much time catching them and arranging them and decorating your room with them. In a few days' time you will be seven years old, and will be starting school."

With one blow the veils were ripped from the boy's consciousness; but by the side of the collection of butterflies in his imagination there arose other collections, vague but attractive, which might be expected to form part of the activities of school.

His cousin Amin, who lived at the other end of the village, was a naughty, mischievous boy, who was likewise in hot water every day; he was more than a year older, and last year he had been enrolled in the primary school in the neighboring town.

In a short time his dress and appearance had changed. His manner of speaking had changed. The way his parents and relations regarded him had changed. He had become a pupil at school and had become, or at any rate was about to become, a grown-up. Now Farid was to be like that. He would probably go to the same school, and would wear the same new uniform, and would have his own small leather satchel. He would have notebooks in it, and pencils, and ink, and paints, and all sorts of secrets, and some butterflies . . . oh, if only butterflies might be flying around the school, even if just once in a while!

His father talked for a long time about school, and duty, and work, and industriousness, and the future, and success in life, and money; but from the outset Farid took in very little of what his father was saying, and finally, as the veils closed over his consciousness ever more thickly, he took in nothing at all.

He spent the night catching butterflies in his sleep. Early next day, when he woke up, he found his father had already gone out. When he asked his mother where he had gone she told him he had gone to town to enroll him at the school and to do some shopping.

He began taking leave of his precious collections of butterflies. He would not have them in a few days' time . . . but why should he not keep some? He would take some of them with him—he would take all of them, wherever he went, wherever he stayed. They were his friends and companions and he could not bear being parted with them. As for those which were still flying around . . . his thoughts yearned toward them and their open spaces; he would not be able to see *them* again. Yet . . . perhaps a way might be found . . .

His heart beat faster, and his imagination flew to all the places and paths which he had been accustomed to haunt in the days past.

There might be a way . . . might he not slip out today and run to see them, to greet them, to say farewell to them for the last time?

It was true he had given a promise to his father yesterday, but it was not really a promise, because it had been forced from him.

Taking advantage of his mother's inattention he got up to go out. He had almost succeeded in slipping out unobserved when at the last moment he heard her call out to him: "Where are you off to, Farid? Have you forgotten what your father said to you yesterday? 'You are not to go out hunting butterflies again.' Have you forgotten your answer and the promise you gave?"

Yes, he was reminded, from today he was a pupil at school, and one day he was to become a man like his cousin . . . and men keep their promises. If they do not, they are not men.

An hour went by, and the heat of the midday became more oppressive. Maybe it caused him to forget—or pretend to forget—everything that had been said by him and to him. He got up and stole quietly out of the house. This time his mother did not notice him slipping through the door, and he was out and away.

Here were *his* paths and tracks, welcoming him with open arms, welcoming him more warmly than his mother . . .

And here were the butterflies, disporting themselves in front of him and around him, challenging him with their lightness, their grace, their joyousness.

There were white ones, yellow ones, variegated ones, brown ones. He had to give chase to them, even if they fluttered to the ends of the earth. He would chase them until he had enough of them for today, for tomorrow, for a whole year. Like a beautiful, love-sick butterfly flying after a fickle, gorgeous mate he ran and chased after them.

But the suffocating heat of summer, which grasped at one's breath; the hot sun which subjected everything to its searching, fiery beams, did not enter into the calculations of the mighty hunter. He set off, ranging further and further afield, until the village was out of sight, and he came upon fields and farms which he had never seen before, nor they him.

Lunch time came, and his father had not arrived home; his mother however was not worried at his being late, as he was usually late if he had not been able to finish all the things that he normally wished to get done.

Lunch time came, and the butterfly collector had not returned home; his mother was anxious and worried at him being late. It was unusual for him to be late for lunch, even if he had been engaged in the chase.

As the late afternoon shadows lengthened, she began to dart anxiously from one balcony to the next, asking news of him, from every neighbor and passer-by, whether she knew them or not.

Just before sunset he was found and carried home. He had gone on chasing butterflies, and on and on, until the sun had overcome him and subdued him with sunstroke. He had been lying in the sun for over an hour. A few hours later he was dead.

The dumb grief which engulfed his stunned mother caused the neighbors and those who had rushed to the house on hearing the news to stand before her and around her speechlessly, afraid to offer even the most restrained condolences.

She refused with terrible unyielding obstinacy to allow his body to be carried away before his father had returned. When he came home tired out with overwork at midnight, bringing the good news of the transformation of the mischievous butterfly collector into a well-behaved schoolboy, the stupefying sight of his silent household performing the solemn funeral rites riveted his eyes. His young wife kept repeating to him in a voice like ashes: "This time your butterfly-catching son went too far . . ."

THE THUNDERBOLT

Zakariyya Tamir

THE CLOUDS DID NOT GO TO SCHOOL in the morning. I commanded the sun not to rise, but it refused to obey me. Accordingly I resolved upon vengeance when I am bigger.

I fixed the math teacher with a stare: he has a face shaped like a triangle. When he noticed me he shouted, "Stand up, boy!"

I stood up, as the teacher continued to address me sternly, showing his disgust, "Stop wiping your nose with your shirt-sleeve!"

I froze, as the teacher continued, "Answer quickly! You have ten million people. You hang seven million. How many people are left alive?"

I answered straightaway, "I don't know."

The teacher replied in exasperation, "How long is your crass ignorance going to continue?"

I answered listlessly: "I hate math."

The teacher's face turned red as he snapped "Oh, so you hate math, do you?" He scowled for a moment. Then he inquired sarcastically, "And what else do you hate? Please enlighten us."

"I hate winter."

"And what else do you hate?"

"I hate winter, summer, autumn, and spring."

"And what else do you hate?"

"I hate day and night."

"And what else do you hate?"

"I hate Saturdays, Sundays, Mondays, Tuesdays, Wednesdays, Thursdays, and Fridays."

"And what else do you hate?"

"I hate the sun, the moon, and the stars."

"And what else do you hate?"

"I hate songs, cats, and birds."

"And what else . . ."

"I hate men. I hate women. I hate children."

At this moment the teacher shouted, "Shut up! You are an incorrigibly ignorant boy!"

I instantly produced an atomic weapon, and flung it as hard as I could. It exploded, and the sun shone down upon rubble.

MADNESS

Abd al-Salam al-Ujayli

i

THE SEASON WAS SUMMER, the time was midday, and the road between Humaymah and Jubb al-Safa, on the way to Aleppo, was empty of cars and people.

The car sped along the asphalt road, but its speed was not enough to cool the hot fiery air which blew against the faces of the car's five occupants. Suddenly the passengers were shot forward in their seats as the car slowed down without warning. The husband, sitting in the rear seat, cried out to his wife: "That's her!"

The driver joined in: "Yes, that's her. That's why I braked. She doesn't usually step off the curb and walk in the middle of the road. I almost ran over her once because I forgot she was mad."

As he said this the car drew level with the subject of their exchange, then quickly left her behind. Everyone except the driver craned around to peer at her. She was wearing a striped dress with a ragged belt. A dark-colored head scarf with a spotted pattern was wound around her head. From under it her hair appeared short, like a man's.

The wife was nearest to her as they passed, and she was able to see clearly her wrinkled, burned, coppery face, with its traces of tatooing. It was a foolish face, the face of a madwoman. All of them observed her peculiar gait. She walked stooping forward, without ever glancing aside to notice what was going on around her, and she walked quickly, as though she were pressing on toward some goal from which neither searing sun nor scorching simoom could deflect her.

The judge, who was occupying the front seat next to the driver, said:

"How is it that they let her go around like this? Why don't they tell the police about her so that they can put her into custody?"

No one answered his question. This was the first time he had opened his mouth since he had gotten into the car at Raqqah. This morning he had reserved both seats next to the driver, so that he would not have to share the front seat with anyone else. Then he had started on his court work quickly and finished it in the late morning. Ensconced in the front seat, he said nothing. He only stirred from time to time to light a cigarette, staring ahead fixedly as though he were listening to a boring submission from some obstinate defense counsel. The silence lasted long enough for the driver to begin to feel embarrassment at no one's answering the judge's question. It was really up to the husband sitting in the back seat to answer, as it was he who had started talking about the madwoman, but he said nothing. The driver said: "But what could the police do with her, Bey? She's been going on like this for twenty years and has never harmed anyone."

The wife joined in: "For twenty years or twenty-five years? You said for twenty-five years, Ahmad."

Her husband returned: "What's the difference? She is mad and that's all there is to it. I've been along this road a thousand times between Aleppo and Raqqah, and I've seen her a thousand times between these two villages, Humaymah and Jubb al-Safa, walking along like this, summer and winter, rain and shine."

In saying this the husband was addressing his wife, but he raised his voice so that the judge should hear. From the start he had been irritated by the haughtiness of the latter. The judge's disdaining to take part in conversation with the other passengers annoyed him, and he had therefore pointedly refrained from answering his question. But he felt the desire for talk coming over him, and he said to himself: "Well, he is a judge after all, always laying down the law in court—he has a right to be a bit distant and proud of himself."

Meanwhile the judge had raised his head and was pretending to puff the smoke from his cigarette into the air. In reality however he was bending his head a little in order to be able to see, in the small mirror in front of the driver, the eyes of the wife, which were looking at him in the same mirror. Two beautiful wide eyes beneath finely arched eyebrows—and the bridge of a delicate nose and two rosy cheeks—were reflected in the mirror.

She was a young woman, and beautiful. She did not seem a fit match for her talkative, paunchy, middle-aged husband, whose clothes bespoke wealth unaccompanied by good taste, and good living unaccompanied by enjoyment.

The fourth passenger spoke. He was a bedouin, who was cloaked in a withdrawal that lay somewhere between pride and uninterest in what was going on. From his appearance he seemed better off than his fellows. He said: "I've been along this road many times, and never seen this poor creature. Or perhaps I have seen her, and no one has been good enough to point out to me that she is out of her mind."

The husband retorted: "It's as I told you. She takes this road every day. She covers the length of it twice between morning and sunset—once going and once returning."

His wife inquired "Why?" without showing much interest, as she was looking into the mirror at the eyes of the youthful judge beneath their thick eyebrows, obscured now and again by ascending puffs of smoke from his cigarette. In the intervals between the puffs she could see the eyes gazing at her in the mirror. They were just the eyes of a man, with nothing remarkable about them. But she noted his youthfulness and elegance later, when the car stopped in front of the law courts and the judge went inside.

Her husband went on: "There are a thousand stories about her. Once, when I was a lorry driver, I gave a lift to a man who lived around here, and he told me the truth of it."

At this point the judge abandoned his air of superiority, and replied to the husband—the eyes of his wife attracted him, and her persistence in looking at him in the mirror gratified him—asking in an ingratiating tone: "And what was the story exactly?"

ii

The husband replied: "It happened when this woman was young. She came from a village near Humaymah. A pretty girl. Twenty-five years ago—and if my wife doesn't like me saying twenty-five years I will say thirty—private cars were few and far between. Only the rich could afford them. One such was the landowner of this village. He was well known for his affairs with women. He caught sight of her on a public holiday, standing with her father on the main road, where they were waiting for a car to take them to her mother's relatives in Jubb al-Safa near Nahr al-Dhahab; and so he gave them a lift in his car.

"He sat them next to the driver, while he sat in the back seat. Her father was one of his tenant-farmers—that's why he gave them a lift."

The wife, with a pertness she had never before shown—at least in public—said: "You said that she was a young girl, Ahmad, and that the Bey was known for his affairs with women. Isn't it more likely he gave them a lift because of her good looks?"

The husband snapped: "Lower your voice, woman! It's true that he had his fair share of entanglements with women, women from all over the place. But not with peasant girls like this one. All the same, I expect you're right. Anyway, the Bey sat in the back and she sat with her father in the front. He kept looking in the mirror—the mirror placed in front of the driver to allow him to see behind—and saw nothing but her eyes in it. You all know how attractive the eyes of some of these peasant girls are. The longer the Bey looked at her the more attractive she seemed. And the wretched girl kept looking—in the mirror—into his eyes."

At this point the eyes of the young wife flickered in the mirror, and the judge noticed she was smiling. His eyes flickered as well—he smiled—while the husband continued his story:

"Since the peasant girl seemed so attractive to the Bey he started a conversation. He asked Abu Abdullah, the girl's father, whether he would be marrying off his son Abdullah soon. The man replied: 'Yes, we are arranging an exchange: I am giving my daughter Khalisah to Husayn, son of Abu Husayn, and I shall take Nu'aymah, daughter of Abu Husayn, for my son Abdullah.' You know the custom of 'exchange marriages' among the country people and the bedouins, and how if one of the two 'exchangees' quarrels with his wife, so that she cannot stand him, or he drives her out, then the other drives out his wife, the sister of the first man—even if there is no reason why she should be driven out. The customs of these people are barbaric."

The voice of the fourth passenger was raised in protest: "And why are our customs barbaric, effendi? You speak as though you townspeople have no objectionable customs whatsoever. Shall I mention a few?"

Making a tactical withdrawal, the husband interrupted him: "I was only speaking about the peasantry. Are you a peasant? You are surely a bedouin of shaykhly family . . . your surely are an Arab shaykh . . ."

The fourth passenger replied: "I'm neither a shaykh nor an agha.* I am like other people, a son of my tribe and my country. Every place has its customs, and people should look at those customs with the eyes of the local people, before saying they are barbarous or quaint. But you townsfolk take no account of people with rough hands. Anyone who works with his hands is not worth twopence as far as you are concerned."

The husband rejoined: "You seem to have taken me seriously, my

---

*Originally a chief officer, military or civil, in the Ottoman Empire; also a title conferred to denote personal distinction. (tr)

dear fellow. All of us work with our hands. I used to be a lorry driver on wages. I was a manual worker and slept rough, in the open. God helped me and I bought my own lorry. Eventually I gained control of a fleet of lorries and tanking facilities. As soon as I'd become a successful man no-one in town looked down on me any more. This girl's people took her from school and married her to me. The great thing is for your pockets to be full—then you will get the prettiest girls of all classes eating out of your hand."

His wife inquired coquettishly: "Whatever do you mean by that, Ahmad?"

Her husband paid no attention to her, but added: "Never mind. Don't take it to heart. Let me finish the story of the madwoman. Now where was I?"

The youthful judge, smiling appreciatively at the tart exchange between the bedouin and the ex-lorry driver—and also at the smiling face of the young woman looking at him in the mirror—responded: "We had reached the discussion of the marriage arrangements between Husayn's father and Abdullah's father."

The husband exclaimed: "Ah yes; well, the Bey asked the father of Abdullah: 'Is this the girl Khalisah you intend to exchange for a wife for your son?' The farmer replied: 'No, this is Jamilah. She is my third daughter.' The Bey then said: 'Why not allow me to give her in marriage?' Abu Abdullah said: 'To whom?' The Bey answered: 'To this chauffeur of mine, sitting beside you—Ishaq. Don't you like the looks of him?' So Abu Abdullah peered at Ishaq, and so did the girl. According to the man who told me the story, this Ishaq was a good-looking chap, with fair hair and blue eyes, and Jamilah liked the looks of him. She stopped staring at the Bey, even in the driving mirror. I know these sheep farmers' girls. I know them well enough, as God is my witness. Before marriage they have the roving eye, but as soon as the question of marriage comes into the picture, or the girl actually gets married, she quiets down."

At this point the fourth passenger broke in maliciously: "Town girls of course are just the opposite: your town girl is quiet and steady-going until she gets a husband—then she gets the roving eye!"

The judge laughed loudly at the fourth passenger's sally, and his laughter was followed by the laughter of the wife, musical and attractive. Her husband chided: "Be quiet, woman! What are you laughing for?"

She returned: "I was laughing because you seem to know the story down to the last detail. You know all about Abu Husayn and Abu Abdullah and Nu'aymah and Khalisah and Jamilah. How can you remember all those names, Ahmad?"

He answered: "Shut up and listen! The girl, as I said, looked at
Ishaq and Ishaq looked at her. He pleased her, and probably she
pleased him. Who knows? We passed through Nahr al-Dhahab a few
moments ago, and here is the village of Jubb al-Safa, the village of
Jamilah's uncles. We are just getting to it. It's around fifteen or twenty
kilometers between this place and Humaymah, and the madwoman
covers them in four or five hours. She wanders on and on and then goes
back to her family's village near Humaymah, getting there before sunset. She sleeps in the village, and then as soon as the sun rises she is on
her way again, back on the road once more. Look, everybody! Here's
the road which turns off to Jubb al-Safa . . . ." And as though staring at
the madwoman the passengers all craned to the left side of the road, trying to descry the village which the husband had indicated. Then they
resumed looking straight ahead, as the car sped on its way to Aleppo.
The eyes of the judge began to peer again into the eyes of the wife in the
mirror, and her eyes looked out at him.

iii

The judge said to himself: "It's now twelve-thirty. Let's say we'll
reach Aleppo by one and be home by one-fifteen. That should be about
right. I shall have enough time to ring up Samiyah before her husband
gets back from work . . . this young woman in the back seat with the
middle-aged windbag of a husband—her eyes are beautiful, very
beautiful. They remind me of Samiyah's eyes . . ."

For the last two or three or even four years this had been the youthful judge's routine. Every Thursday he conveniently calculated his
arrival in Aleppo before the government offices had closed their doors
and the civil servants had left to go home, so that he could telephone
Samiyah. This had been simple when his court was at Idlib—it was
only a short distance away, and most of the civil servants (many of
whose families lived in Aleppo) had come to a mutual understanding to
knock off work on Thursdays by as much as an hour before the official
end of office hours. But it was more difficult in his new post. He had to
travel two hundred kilometers to reach Aleppo. Certainly this distance
did not seem so much, when he imagined himself listening to Samiyah's
voice and talking to her, and her talking to him, and the idea that he
might see her on the road, or might visit her at her home, or perhaps . . .
perhaps she might meet him at the other house. When he imagined all
this any distance dwindled and disappeared. But work . . . it was very
difficult to abandon litigants and adjourn cases in order to get from his

office in Raqqah to his house in Aleppo, before the civil servants there had traveled from their offices to their homes.

Nevertheless he had managed to do this on frequent Thursdays since his transfer—as on this Thursday. He had traveled the road every day, back and forth, between Humaymah and Jubb al-Safa. He traversed it just as she did, though for a different purpose . . . for a purpose which usually demands a great deal of traveling and rushing from pillar to post . . . and what purpose could compare with Samiyah's eyes?

How strange is life, how short are distances, how peculiar are human desires! When he was studying law in Damascus he was attracted to this girl Samiyah, but never dared to speak to her. He used to see her at the students' club, and he would look at her and she would look at him. He would say to himself: "A lot of men have their eyes on her, but does she give any of them a second glance?"

He convinced himself that she looked at no one but himself—or at least that she looked at others but not in the same way as she looked at him. It was pure imagination and self-deception. But he derived satisfaction from such thoughts and beguiled himself with them. Then their ways parted. They no longer came across each other in the students' club, the footpaths of the university garden or the colonnades of the Faculty of Law. Then one day he met her by chance in his home town of Aleppo.

By this time he had already become a probationary judge, and she was now married and had come with her husband to the city. She gave a shout when she saw him. He felt his heart jump violently, and then beat rapidly, turning his face scarlet and reddening his ears. They shook hands and chatted and he told her what had transpired since he left the university. She told him where she lived, and gave him her telephone number. All this was the result of one chance meeting in the covered Arcade of Awqaf, in front of the shoemaker's shop at the corner.

In the days that followed the judge discovered, during the long moments that the two of them spent on the telephone, that he loved Samiyah. And as they conversed with each other, that discovery became more and more firmly rooted in his mind. And Samiyah? She told him that he had often attracted her attention. True, she had not been thinking of love, but if her heart had desired anyone at that time it would have been him. But however that might have been, she had never loved anyone since. Her marriage was a marriage of convenience; or, to put it differently, they were meant for each other, as people say.

Now what were they to do since discovering from one meeting and numerous telephone calls that they were in love—that each loved the other? She had become a wife with two small children, while he had remained single and had never thought about marriage, until now. If only he had summoned up enough courage to speak to her during their time at the university . . . if he had spoken they would have dated each other; if they had dated they would have become engaged; if they had become engaged they would have married. If . . . but what use was there in "if"?

He met her again. Talks over the telephone were followed by meetings—in the street, the park, and once in a car which one of his friends lent him. He took her for a tour around the city after dark. They had stopped at a certain spot on the road and looked down at Aleppo beneath them, and she gazed on the lights of the city gathered into clusters, or set out in strings like the beads of a rosary, all twinkling like stars on a moonlit night.

She said: "Look at the lights in the windows of the houses and the buildings. They belong to people just like us—but they are able to love each other in the light—you and I can only love in the darkness!"

Her hand had been in his as she said these words. He had drawn her toward him and wrapped his arm around her shoulders. Then he let it fall to her waist, and he kissed her for the first time.

And after that? After that he had paid her fleeting visits on many occasions during the day and she had given him coffee. After that she had called on him one evening, at the house of a bachelor friend which was in a quarter of Aleppo known as al-Sabil, on a dark back street What an evening that had been! He still remembered its happiness— and its torment. Samiyah, a married woman who had two children by a husband with whom she still lived, even though she did not love him; and he, a judge, a supporter of the sword of justice, who must come down firmly on those who transgress the law, and stray from the path of morality . . .

She and he had come together that evening: two people who knew quite well what they should do and should not do, yet who had come together as lovers, alone in a small house all to themselves. In a corner of the room there had been a record player and some classical records, and in another a bar furnished with a variety of drinks. In another room was a cozy bed, on one side of which stood a bronze statuette. Below it they read the name of the sculpture: "Eternal Spring," by Rodin. It was of a naked girl and a youth. Their lips were united in a passionate kiss, while their bodies were suffused with eager desire. And here they were, the two of them, alone in that house after months and years of waiting and dreaming of a love that was forbidden . . .

From that evening onward the young judge had lived in both heaven and hell at the same time: the heaven of mutual love and the hell of illicit courtship. Ever since, wherever he was, he had been in a hurry to be on his way to Aleppo, to reach her before the master of the house returned, to pour out his passion; eager to arrange a meeting in the park, or on the street, or under the eye of "Eternal Spring." And here he was today traveling in this car with these fellow passengers for this very purpose. Was it a purpose? Here was this man's wife sitting behind him, eyeing him enticingly—yet she did nothing but remind him of Samiyah. It was true that she had attracted his attention just as that peasant girl had attracted the attention of the Bey, but what possible connection could he ever have with this traveling beauty with her husband sitting beside her? He did not know what the Bey had done with the peasant girl, but he knew that no woman could take Samiyah's place in his heart, or arouse his emotions as she did. Wherever his official post took him, wherever circumstances took him, he would return to the place where Samiyah was. He would travel the roads back and forth, just as that mad peasant girl traveled the roads in pursuit of . . . in pursuit of what?

He had better listen to the end of that story about the madwoman, from the lips of the talkative, portly husband . . .

iv

After the car had passed the turn-off to Jubb al-Safa the husband resumed his story: "I told you that the girl Jamilah was attracted to the Bey's chauffeur; and the idea of marriage entered her head. And it was more firmly fixed there when the Bey returned with his car by the same road three or four days later, and found the girl in front of her uncle's house waiting for someone to take her back to her village. Who can say? She may have been waiting there all that time for the Bey's black car and his chauffeur Ishaq, with his fair hair. Anyway, the Bey recognized her and offered her a lift, inviting her to sit beside the chauffeur. On this occasion she was by herself, and the Bey starting talking about marriage again. Like any modest girl, Jamilah made no answer. But imagine what might stir in the mind of a girl when the local squire talked about marrying her to a fair-haired, fresh-faced young man like Ishaq, who wore a smart suit and turned the driving wheel as though he had been born with it between his hands!

"Jamilah was dazzled by this talk, and replied with a blush and a flutter of her eyelashes. Ishaq smiled at his master's remarks, and at the naiveté of the girl sitting beside him, averting her glance at one moment and stealing a look at his face the next. Some say that Ishaq's smile was a smile of approval, not of mockery, and that he had told the Bey that he would have wished to marry Jamilah, were he not aware that the bridal money of girls in these villages was more than he could afford from his modest wages.

"They say that the Bey undertook to pay Jamilah's nuptial gift himself, and that he stopped the car and put the girl's hand in Ishaq's, and promised that he would come around at 'Id al-Fitr and ask for her hand from Abu Abdullah. Some people say this, and that a good many other things happened in the Bey's car between the two villages that day.

"Perhaps the whole business was a joke for the Bey to amuse himself with while touring around his estates in that area. But what happened afterwards was not amusing: everybody has heard of the disaster which overtook the Bey's car on the road to Beirut, just outside Tripoli. There is a dangerous curve there which overlooks the sea as you approach the tunnel. The car skidded and toppled over the edge. Not a trace of the car or its owner or the chauffeur remained."

The wife exclaimed: "Oh my God! Did they fall into the sea?"

Her husband returned: "Yes, and they have never been recovered. The story of the accident was the main topic of conversation for a long time in those parts, and especially in the villages owned by the Bey, particularly in the village of Abu Abdullah, the father of the girl Jamilah. People were upset by this accident which had killed the Bey, and they said prayers for his soul, remembering his good qualities and disregarding his bad ones. He had been a rich man, with a knack for getting his own way; at times a warm-hearted man, at others a harsh man; but now he had passed on to a higher judgment, as everyone said, privately and publicly—except Jamilah.

"Jamilah would not believe that the Bey was dead, or that the car and her Ishaq who had been driving it had plunged into the sea on the Tripoli road and never been seen again. She believed that the Bey would not lie, in spite of all the disparaging things that the village people might say about him. He had promised her he would come and arrange the engagement with her father . . . therefore he must be coming, must be coming in his black car, sitting in the back seat, allowing her to sit beside Ishaq."

The wife broke in: "The poor soul! How could she believe a man!"

The judge, apparently finding an opportunity to address the wife directly, asked: "Don't you believe men then?"

The wife laughed briskly and prepared to argue with the youthful judge, but her husband cut her off, resuming the story: "A slow-witted peasant girl. In her eyes the Bey was a man who could not be defeated by anything, even death."

Here the fourth passenger cleared his throat, and the husband, guessing he was about to protest this description, forestalled him by elaborating on his portayal: "The poor girl knew nothing of worldly affairs. She had little experience. The point is that she did not believe the Bey and his chauffeur were dead. Secretly she went on waiting for the car and the chauffeur and the Bey, at first at home and later in the street. She would tell her family that she intended to visit her mother's brothers in Jubb al-Safa, and if they suggested she should take a hire-car going along the main road in the direction of her uncles' village, she always refused, remaining in the road, whatever the weather. She would stand for hours and hours, and would only return home after the cajolings and sometimes threats of her family.

"Gradually the secret of Abu Abdullah's daughter Jamilah came out: she was waiting for the Bey's black car driven by the fair-haired Ishaq to drive her to her uncles' village and then bring her back again. Jamilah began after a time to walk along the main road, in the direction of Jubb al-Safa . . . she hailed every black car, coming or going, and if the car stopped she would peer at the people inside. Then she would trudge on her way. At first she would walk on only a little way, then some hundreds of meters, then for some kilometers, then the whole distance to Jubb al-Safa and back . . ."

The husband said no more, regaining his breath after his lengthy account. The fourth passenger spoke up: "She was a poor soul right enough! But her family—what did they do about it? How could they allow their daughter to wander alone along lonely roads?"

With genuine concern the wife exclaimed: "How weak we women are! Who would have thought that a few words spoken in jest would have brought all this on the girl?"

The judge delivered his opinion: "She cannot have lost her reason simply because of the promise of marriage, a promise which had not been confirmed. The family should have conducted a closer investigation of what happened on the road between the girl on the one hand and the Bey and his chauffeur on the other."

The fourth passenger answered him: "You are quite right, your honor. God forbid that we should think the worst. But this matter was no trifling affair. People are tough. They do not lose their minds for trifles."

At this point the driver broke in: "The human mind is like hard crystal. It can scratch even steel, but it can be smashed by simply dropping it on the ground. Do you honestly think that the people you see all around are sound in their heads? There are an awful lot of unsuspected madmen in the streets. This girl's madness just happened to make her stand out from the rest . . ."

The fourth passenger assented: "Perfectly true, cousin*—but I tell you . . ."

v

The fourth passenger fell silent before he had finished his sentence. He had had it in mind to say something, but he was afraid it might slight the judge. He had intended to say something insulting about townsfolk in general, but the judge was one of them; so he said nothing. He had been on the verge of saying that the girl had not lost her reason because she was involved with a young man whom she had lost, since being crazed by love was unknown to country people. It was a sickness of young men and girls of the towns, with their weak minds and silly emotions. In the countryside and villages love may be the reason for murder, but never for madness . . .

The truth was that the fourth passenger, in saying this—if he had said it—would have had only one object in mind: to pick a quarrel with this town-dweller who was telling the story of the mad Jamilah. Had he been quite fair, he would have acknowledged that the Sultan of Love lends his ear to everyone, and extends his favor to countryfolk and townsfolk alike, bestowing sometimes happiness and sometimes misery, and in sundry places bringing men finally to madness.

But perhaps the truth was that the fourth passenger had reached an age and a condition in which he regarded the emotion which bound a youth to a maid as being too trifling to cause either to lose their reason.

If it were not for his having taken this car, which had forced on him this company and this conversation to which he had been unable to close his ears, listening to the babble of the townsman would have been the last thing he would have endured, for all the man's elegant tone. Nor would he have endured the laughter of his wife, a brazen hussy for all her beautiful features. This was because the thoughts of the fourth passenger were preoccupied with worries of his own; they did not have room for this babble, and this shamelessness . . .

Ever since this passenger had taken his seat in the car, he had been asking himself: would he be able to catch up with the man who, he had been told, knew the haunts of Mashhur al-Dalman? He had learned the man had been in Aleppo for some days, and that he frequented a stall at

---

*A form of address in Arabic implying intimacy or sympathy, without necessarily indicating any relationship. (tr)

the entrance of Suq al-Zarb in the city market. He was known by the name of his place of work, and was a dealer in hides, ropes, and fencing materials. He bought these on behalf of Mashhur al-Dalman, who lived somewhere in the country between Najd and Jordan, or between Najd and Iraq, or somewhere in the Badiyat al-Sham. Thus there was nothing between the fourth passenger and finding Mashhur except an interview with this man; and then the worries of years, the fires of hatred, and the numerous long journeys would have an end.

The fourth passenger would not have recognized Mashhur al-Dalman even if he had seen him. He had only been a child when Mashhur al-Dalman had attacked his tribe; and that was the only thing that had saved him from the fate of all his elder tribesmen: death.

Now conditions had changed, and time had moved on. No one carries out armed raids on peaceful bedouin encampments any longer, or carries off sheep and camels, or slaughters innocent people wholesale. However, a chance dispute between two women had roused memories of the old days of lawless raiding, and had stirred up old emotions. One of these women was the wife of the fourth passenger. He had heard the other woman saying to his wife: "You keep telling us about your husband and his wealth. If you had a real man for a husband, he would not have spent all his time enlarging his herds and selling lard and wool, while the man who murdered his father and uncle and brother lived only a stone's throw away—Mashhur al-Dalman!"

But the truth was that Mashhur al-Dalman was not living a stone's throw away; he was nowhere to be found, and was in fact not in the country at all. But the rebuke had been uttered and the fourth passenger could no longer sleep at night. It had made his life, which had to this point been happy, intolerable. He had now become the eternal wanderer in search of vengeance; he had no fixed abode.

Where would this implacable avenger track down Mashhur al-Dalman? Everyone knew the usual encampments of Mashhur's tribe; but the passenger could not be satisfied with merely harming the tribe—he wanted Mashhur himself, and Mashhur had not been in this country for years. Lean years and seasons of drought would bring him to the borders of the irrigated lands on the plains of al-Jazirah and the Euphrates; at other times he would range across remote deserts as far as the Empty Quarter of Arabia. Mashhur had ceased to camp in this country ever since laws and regulations had been imposed upon it; it was now under the control of a police force and Desert Guards mounted on armored cars using wireless communications. This may have been partly due to fear of the consequences of deeds he had perpetrated in the past; but principally it was a result of the rebellious spirit of al-Dalman and his ilk, which shunned restraint and authority.

On one occasion the fourth passenger had heard that his enemy had settled in a certain locality in the wilderness, a featureless site on the desert frontier, where he smuggled prohibited goods, tobacco, weapons, drugs, tires, and sugar to and from Kuwait, Aqabah, Saudi Arabia, and Iraq.

It was reported to him that a trap was going to be set by government forces against one of the smuggling caravans which al-Dalman protected in person. Accordingly the fourth passenger accompanied the expedition and was involved in an armed clash in which he had shown himself more daring than the government troops. The caravan had stumbled into the ambush, and three of its men had been wounded, but al-Dalman had vanished after shooting two customs officers.

The fourth passenger had escaped unharmed from a shot which tore his clothes but failed to graze his body. He had almost been killed in his unfulfilled quest; and once more he resumed his chase down every path that might lead him to his prey. That had been but one occasion; there had been many others.

He would continue to gather news of Mashhur al-Dalman and pursue him, while the latter avoided his net like a drop of quicksilver. He was aware that al-Dalman had no fear of a fight, but the malefactor still evaded the avenger's wrath. How long would this evasion succeed? One day they would meet face to face, and in expectation of this encounter the fourth passenger imprinted the days with his steps, tracing and retracing. Compared with this quest, of what importance could the madwoman's trudging back and forth on the highway be, in pursuit of her fatuous, imaginary aim?

"Fatuous, imaginary aim, what else?" said the fourth passenger to himself. As for *his* aim . . .

vi

The fourth passenger was of the opinion that it was impossible for the village girl to have lost her reason merely on account of the chauffeur to whom the Bey had promised to marry her. The judge had agreed with his expression of doubt, or rather he had agreed with the judge. The husband, who had told the story, insisted on holding to his view of the matter. "She was only a simple girl, as I told you; she didn't have much experience or knowledge of the world . . . she was not very intelligent; clutched at a straw . . . I know women."

Having delivered himself of these sentiments he subsided. He certainly was acquainted with women, for he had six daughters, the eldest of whom was the same age as the wife beside him. He was still married to his first wife, but he had deserted her in despair of her ever bearing him a male child. Or was this merely an excuse for deserting the poor creature and running after a girl who, although he had made her his wife, was no older than his daughter?

Indeed, he was still chasing his wife, because she constantly slipped away from him. On one pretext or another she was forever going off visiting, or traveling, or sulking, or pretending to be ill. On this trip he was bringing her back from her sister's house. She had gone there on a week's visit, and the week had lengthened to almost a month. If he had not gone to fetch her in person her visit would certainly have been prolonged indefinitely.

When he got into the car at Aleppo to bring her back he kept asking himself what his wife had found at her sister's to make her so extend her visit. Her sister's husband was a minor civil servant in Raqqah. In his house were neither the space nor the gracious accommodations which she could enjoy in her own husband's house. He had denied her nothing; he had installed her in different quarters so that she would not be living with his first wife and their daughters; he had bought her new furniture when she had refused what she described as throw-aways from the old house; he had bought her the television set for which his daughters had long begged, and which he had long refused on the grounds that times were bad and he could not afford it.

In spite of all this, Nazmiyyah, this new wife of his, would not settle in this house which he had equipped with everything she could ever desire. Every time he returned from one of his trips he found her at her family's home in the Banqusa quarter, or with one of her married sisters in the eastern part of town; or he would not find her in Aleppo at all. Her family would tell him that she was paying a visit miles away— today it was Raqqah, a couple of months ago it was with her aunt in Hims.

When her people had told him that day that she was in Hims, and that her cousin, a driver employed by one of his rivals, had taken her there in his car, he lost his head in blind fury—the fury of jealousy. He had not forgotten that Nazmiyyah had been engaged to her cousin before he came along and snatched her away with his money to become his wife. How on earth could her family agree to let her accompany her cousin all the way to Hims, to stay with her aunt and the family of her former betrothed? How on earth could she go? That night he had almost lost his mind. However, he had found comfort by telling himself that her cousin was no more than a brother to her in view of her marriage to him. He was sure that Nazmiyyah was innocent of the behavior of which he had at first been suspicious. In spite of her flirtatious manner, her beckoning eyes and sly smile and the way she had of slowly cracking mastic with her teeth, she was still only a child no older than his eldest daughter. She would not behave as more mature women might behave when smitten by desire for a man. She was his wife . . . he was on intimate terms with her. He knew how shy and inexperienced and ignorant she was in these matters.

Nazmiyyah had returned with him from Hims on that occasion without protest. She had displayed no opposition to returning, and her husband's suspicions were thus banished all the more quickly. But she was soon slipping away again. She tired him out. If only a baby boy would arrive and relieve him of the need to chase after this girl, with her constant attempts to fly off. He wondered whether she would even settle when she had a baby. He wondered whether he would ever be able to rest from this tiresome business. It was as though he were a Jamilah, forever running toward a goal and returning every day empty-handed and frustrated, and then resuming the chase the following day.

He sighed as this passed through his mind, and then, emerging from his silence, he addressed the judge: "Yes, I know all about women . . . and I don't believe what a certain person once told me—someone else, not our fellow passenger here—the man who gave me the first account of the story."

His wife broke in: "What did a certain person tell you, Ahmad?"

In an exasperated tone, as though his brooding on her going off with her cousin had hardened him toward her, he snapped at her: "You be quiet. I am telling the story to the gentleman. No, I didn't believe this other fellow when he said that the peasant girl did not return to her village on the same day that the Bey and the chauffeur took her. At that time cars were rarities and communications were not very good. How could Jamilah's family know whether their daughter had left her uncles' place that day or the day before? That's what this chap said. May God judge between us if the girl did not return to the village—which is near Humaymah—a whole day after leaving Jubb al-Safa, and passed a whole night and part of the next day in the company of the Bey and his chauffeur Ishaq. Where might that have been? The Bey had a house on its own grounds in one of his villages, miles away from the main road. He used to go there with his foreign acquaintances and his actress friends, and there was a cottage for the chauffeur there as well. Did the girl spend the night in the house or the cottage? No one knows. This fellow said that the girl never spoke a word when she went back home. When the news spread three days later that the Bey's car had been lost in the sea near Tripoli with him and the chauffeur in it, she ran the

124

whole way from Humaymah to Jubb al-Safa and spent the night at her uncles'. The next day she ran back the whole way from Jubb al-Safa to Humaymah. He said that the secret of her madness lies in what happened that night. Just imagine: a girl of seventeen, a great big house and a cottage, with a lady-killing lord and a strapping young man with blue eyes, of whose real character nobody knows a thing . . ."

vii

After saying this, the husband fell silent again, and no one ventured to comment on the narrative of the "other" narrator. Although he had not gone into much detail about what had taken place, or about what the man thought had taken place, the manner of the husband's alluding to the conversation strongly suggested what in all probability *had* taken place.

The fourth passenger said to himself: "Confound these townspeople! If this business really happened then the whole thing is disgusting. If it didn't happen then the suggestiveness of these people is revolting. They've no shame and no fear of God!"

The judge's mind was agitated by the thought of the apparent violation of a gullible girl by two unscrupulous men whom she trusted. But his imagining an empty house with a girl all alone recalled an empty house with a woman all alone—a woman to whom he had given the key so that she could let herself in while she waited for him. The resemblance was uncomfortably close between this house and the other, between the girl and the woman, between the girl's circumstances and the woman's; but the youthful judge's thoughts evoked other connections whose nature he did not fully grasp. Then the agitation within him calmed down, and became a feeling of impatience which would not be stilled by feelings of guilt, nor deadened by a premonition of impending danger.

The young wife, Nazmiyyah, looked at her husband after he had finished retelling the "other man's" story, with wide eyes which had a strange look in them. Her husband said that he didn't believe the story, yet he obviously relished telling it. Here he was, casting suspicion on the Bey, but she was quite certain in her own mind that what had happened—if anything had happened—had nothing to do with the Bey. She imagined that it was something between Jamilah and Ishaq. Something between a strong, handsome young man and a beautiful girl. She turned away from her husband and threw her head back with her eyes closed. Normally she thought little, and had a dull imagination. But her husband's story had agitated a strange feeling, stirred up by the images which filled her mind. She thought that the madwoman was not Jamilah, the peasant girl, but herself, Nazmiyyah. It was she who was running along the road in vain, seeking something she had lost. Now she was able to recognize what she had lost, and until now had not been able to secure. It was her cousin, or her love for her cousin.

When he had accompanied her on that journey to Hims, the car had been empty but for her. He took no passengers with him, even though he had paid the car's owner the fares of five passengers out of his own pocket. During the early part of the journey, between Aleppo and Hims, the two of them had talked a great deal. They had talked innocuously about their childhood and about his brothers and sisters and their mothers, and she had talked about her husband. Then they both fell silent.

After they had passed through Ma'arrah they reached a winding road which wound around a small hurst, and he leaned against her as he turned the car to follow the road. When the road straightened out again she leaned against him, and he embraced her with such force that the car almost leaped across the shoulder at the edge of the roadway. She had not resisted the embrace, but had yielded to it, and as a result the journey took longer—but seemed to be over more quickly.

Now, traveling beside her husband, she thought of that day and that embrace. Did not Jamilah have every cause to lose her reason in her search for Ishaq? Here she was, Nazmiyyah, almost going out of her mind, almost going crazy in her desire for her cousin—even in just thinking about him. She was returning unsuccessfully to Aleppo like the mad Jamilah going back to Humaymah . . . going back to her husband! How could she share the bed of this corpulent man with his malodorous breath and heavy snoring? She had begun to hate men the first time she got into his bed: all men, when she felt him lay his hand on her and draw her toward him, naked, calling to her with shameless words and vile gestures.

But when her cousin had put his arm around her in the car as they raced along, and when he had stopped the car and touched her, running his hand over her breasts and thighs, and when her eager body had nestled against his sturdy form, she loved manhood and men and felt a great joy at being a woman, feminine . . .

Yes, she was crazy, like Jamilah, and would remain so.

The silence of the passengers in the car lengthened, until they were soon nearing Aleppo. The driver announced: "We're here. I expect you'll be going home or going on to your business engagements. I'll be going back again. I shall have a bit of a rest and then return by the same route—like Jamilah! I travel to and fro just like her, but my errand has less significance. She's looking for someone she loves that she's lost, but what am I looking for?"

The judge remarked drily: "You're earning your family's daily bread."

The driver sighed, and then in the tone of one whose patience is exhausted, replied: "Earning my family's daily bread or money to pay for my girlfriend at the pub, what's the difference? I beg your pardon, lady, for my manner of speaking. But whatever it is I'm looking for I come back empty-handed. Night and day I'm tearing around between one town and another after dirty bits of colored paper. And every time I think I've got my hands on them they just evaporate and slip away like water between my fingers. I'm more mad than she is, that Jamilah. Journeys, journeys, journeys, there and back again the whole time."

The judge replied: "If it's a question of journeying, we are all on a journey. All our life is taken up coming and going—the outbound journey and the homecoming."

The driver returned: "My dear Bey, when you travel you enjoy respect and prestige, and by traveling you expect to gain more respect and prestige. Soon I expect you will be made president of the court of cassation—then perhaps a minister. But the likes of me do nothing but run after illusions, like Jamilah. If I let my attention wander from the road for just a moment the same thing would happen to me as almost happened to her once, when I nearly ran her over."

The judge raised his eyes to the mirror, where they once more met the eyes of the young wife—she had roused herself from her dejected pose with her head on the headrest—but her eyes were wide open, with no trace of flirtatiousness. Perhaps, like him, she was absorbed in her thoughts.

He was pondering over the driver's delusions—his saying that he, the judge, traveled to increase his respect and prestige. What respect, what prestige? He was traveling to find Samiyah, to seek Samiyah's love. He had to roam streets in which hidden hazards lurked. If he stepped falsely, a disaster might overwhelm him and rob him of his position or even of his life. He might be killed by a bullet from a jealous husband; there might be a scandal, which would just as surely destroy his career; or on the other hand Samiyah's leaving him, or the withering of his love for her, might finish him off. Despite it all he was just like the driver, like Jamilah, continually running after something that was of the world of illusions . . . illusions based on the fantasies of the vanished past, or of vanished pleasures, which he fondly imagined could continue into the present, or last into the future . . .

The fourth passenger spoke: "Are we going to stop at the City

Market near Suq al-Zarb?"

The driver laughed. "Surely you know Aleppo! Suq al-Zarb is right off our track. I've got to stop at the garage to book my arrival time. The City Market is not far to walk from there, especially if you're used to walking across deserts. Just imagine yourself like Jamilah, walking between Humaymah and Jubb al-Safa twice a day."

The fourth passenger was not amused by the driver's pleasantry. "What has that crazy woman got to do with it? God ordained she should be so. Who knows? Her fate may be easier than ours. We are all wayfarers on one road . . . people on the road to Jubb al-Safa, to al-Dayr, to Ma'arrah . . ."

At the mention of the road to Ma'arrah the young wife felt a longing that caused her to melt inwardly. If only that road, the road to Ma'arrah, had been blocked at that turn-off! If only her cousin had dragged her to that hut which was at the side of the road! Then she would have spent a night in the hut, like the night Jamilah spent with Ishaq, and her madness would have some precious, significant experience as its origin. Her present madness was spawned only from deprivation.

Her husband spoke up: "Before you get to the garage take us past the quarter around Baghdad Station—our house is not far off your route."

The driver replied: "As you please. We owe you something for your amusing story about the madwoman. It seems to me I'm just like her. As our friend here says, there are many mad people on the roads, but the roads vary."

The husband returned: "May God keep you in your right mind. I used to be a driver, the same as you—only a lorry driver, which is a good deal tougher. I traveled many routes, longer than yours. And have I gone mad? The man who has money, my dear chap, does not go mad, and if he does go crazy for money—well, the more crazy for money, the more sense he's got."

The driver laughed as the car plunged into the crowded streets of Aleppo, and, adroitly turning the wheel to avoid a fast-moving lorry, said: "Please yourself. I'll pray to the good Lord to increase your wealth—I mean to increase your madness."

All joined in the driver's laughter. Nazmiyyah laughed loudly and hysterically, but artificially and without amusement. The judge gave a short mirthless laugh. Even the fourth passenger cleared his throat loudly to mask a malicious guffaw. Then the laughter quickly died away into the din of the city and the heat of midday. The people in the streets jostled and pushed amid uproar and clamor, as though all of them were mad.

NOTES ON THE AUTHORS

ABDULLAH ABID: born in 1935 in Latakia; died in 1976. He was employed in the Government Department of Tobacco. He published two collections of short stories.

JOHN ALEXAN: born in 1935 in al-Hasaka. He is co-editor of the daily newspaper *Al-Ba'th*. Apart from his work as a journalist he is active as an author of short stories, plays, and literary criticism. He has published three collections of short stories and a collection of plays entitled *Masrah al-Ma'rakah* ("Theater of battle"), 1977. He has also published an important history of the Arab cinema.

ULFAT AL-IDLIBI: born in 1912 in Damascus. One of the most distinguished women writers of present-day Syria, she began writing in the 1950s and has published three collections of short stories, together with works of literary criticism. Among the latter is her book *Nazrah fi Adabina al-Sha'bi* ("An Examination of our popular literature"), 1974.

HAYDAR HAYDAR: born in 1936 in Tartous. He worked in Algeria for a number of years, and was a school teacher until 1962. He has published many short stories and a novel, *Al-Zaman al-Mutawahhish* ("Savage time"), 1974.

SA'ID HURANIYYAH: born in 1929 in Damascus. He holds a B.A. in Arabic Studies and has worked as a teacher in both Syria and Lebanon. He is a prolific writer who has published short stories, essays, and plays.

WALID IKHLASI: born in 1935 in Alexandretta. He holds a Bachelor's degree in Agricultural Science, but has also found time to

130

make important contributions to literature. He is widely recognized as being one of the most outstanding contemporary writers in Arabic, who has published short stories, novels, and plays. His novels include *Shita al-Bahr al-Yabis* ("Winter of the dry sea"), 1975; and his plays include *Al-Sirat* ("The Path"), 1976, and the collection *Sab'ah Aswat Khashinah* ("Seven rough voices"), 1979.

COLETTE KHURI: born in 1937 in Damascus. She is a lecturer at the University of Damascus who has published novels and short stories as well as articles in the daily press. She has also published collections of poems originally composed in French. Her novels include *Ayyam Ma'ahu* ("Days with him"), 1959, and *Laylah Wahidah* ("One night"), 1960.

SABAH MUHYI 'L-DIN: born in 1925, died in 1962. He held a B.A. in English from the University of London and a Ph.D. in French from the Sorbonne. He worked as a journalist in Aleppo and Beirut. He published three collections of short stories and a novel, *Khamr al-Shabab* ("Wine of youth").

HANI AL-RAHIB: born in 1939 in Latakia. A lecturer in English at the University of Damascus, he has published short stories and novels, and has also translated works of English literature into Arabic.

YASIN RIFA'IYYAH: born in 1939 in Damascus. He left school early. His first published work appeared in 1958. He has written many short stories and poems; a novel, *Al-Mamarr* ("The Corridor"), 1978; and a collection of stories for children, entitled *The Birds Search for a Homeland.*

GEORGE SĀLIM: born in 1933, died in 1976. A graduate of the University of Damascus, he worked as a civil servant in the Ministry of Culture. He published a novel, two plays, and many short stories, including the two outstanding collections *Al-Rahil* ("The Departure") and *Hiwar al-Summ* ("Dialogue of the deaf"). He also wrote a critical study of the development of the Arabic novel, *Al-Mughamarah al-Riwa'iyyah* ("The Venture of the novel").

GHADAH AL-SAMAN: born in 1942 in Damascus. She graduated from the University of Damascus. She has worked as a lecturer and a journalist, and now owns a publishing house in Beirut. She has published poems and short stories, and two novels, *Beirut 75* and *Kawabis Bayrut* ("Nightmares of Beirut").

FU'AD AL-SHAYIB: born in 1910, died in 1970. He studied law in Damascus and Paris, and published a collection of short stories entitled *Tarikh Jarh* ("History of a wound").

FADIL AL-SIBA'I: born in 1929 in Aleppo. He graduated in law and became a lawyer. He has published seven collections of short stories and three novels.

NABIL SULAYMAN: born in 1945 in Latakia. He holds a B.A. in Arabic from the University of Damascus and was a secondary school teacher until 1979, when he established a publishing house under the name of *Dar al-Hiwar.* He is primarily a novelist, and has published some literary criticism: *Literary Criticism in Syria* (1980) and *The Syrian Novel* (1982).

MUZAFFAR SULTAN: born in 1913 in Aleppo. He studied for a degree in Cairo, and then worked as a teacher. His published works include two collections of short stories, *Damir al-Dhi'b* ("The Wolf's conscience"), 1960, and *Fintizar al-Masir* ("Awaiting fate"), 1976.

ZAKARIYYA TAMIR: born in 1931 in Damascus. One of the most distinguished Syrian authors writing today, he began writing in the late 1950s and has been editor of the important literary magazine *Al-Ma'rifah.* Among his many works are three collections of short stories and two books of stories for children, *Qalat al-Wardah li'l-Sununu* ("The Rose said to the swallow"), 1977, and *Bilad al-Aranib* ("The Land of the rabbits"), 1979.

ABD AL-SALAM AL-UJAYLI: born in Raqqah, c. 1918. A Doctor of Medicine who has a clinic in Raqqah, his very large literary production includes poetry, plays, short stories, novels, and many essays. He is widely recognized as one of the leading Syrian authors of today. His best-known collections of short stories include *Dima fi 'l-Subh al-Aghbar* ("Blood in the dusty morning") and *Al-Tin* ("Clay").